The Path to Forever

ROSEWOOD PRESS

Print ISBN: 979-8-9904728-6-0

The Path to Forever

Copyright © 2025 by Megan Leavell

All rights reserved. Except for the use of brief quotations in review of this novel, no part of this book may be reproduced in any form or by any electronic or mechanical means, including information storage and retrieval systems, without written permission from the author.

This is a work of fiction. Names, characters, businesses, places, events and incidents are either the products of the author's imagination or used in a fictitious manner. Any resemblance to actual persons, living or dead, or actual events is purely coincidental.

Also by Olivia Miles

Harmony Cove

Home Sweet Harmony

Stand Alone Titles

Find Me in Paris

The Gift of Christmas

The Starlight Sisters

A Wedding in Driftwood Cove

The Heirloom Inn

Christmas in Winter Lake

Sunrise Sisters

A Memory So Sweet

A Promise to Keep

A Wish Come True

Evening Island

Meet Me at Sunset

Summer's End

The Lake House

The Sweeter in the City Series

Sweeter in the Summer

Sweeter Than Sunshine

No Sweeter Love

One Sweet Christmas

The Blue Harbor Series

A Place for Us

Second Chance Summer

Because of You

Small Town Christmas

Return to Me

Then Comes Love

Finding Christmas

A New Beginning

Summer of Us

A Chance on Me

The Misty Point Series

One Week to the Wedding

The Winter Wedding Plan

The Oyster Bay Series

Feels Like Home

Along Came You

Maybe This Time

This Thing Called Love

Those Summer Nights

Christmas at the Cottage

Still the One

One Fine Day

Had to Be You

The Briar Creek Series

Mistletoe on Main Street

A Match Made on Main Street

Hope Springs on Main Street

Love Blooms on Main Street

Christmas Comes to Main Street

Harlequin Special Edition

'Twas the Week Before Christmas

Recipe for Romance

The Path to Forever

HARMONY COVE
BOOK TWO

OLIVIA MILES

Ⓡ

One

Caroline Baker didn't do weddings. She didn't plan them. She didn't attend them. She certainly didn't participate in them. Yet here she was, fluffing an ivory tulle veil as her client took her father's arm. Caroline listened carefully to the music, knowing from the rehearsal that right about now the rather pokey flower girl should be finishing her walk and that the lantern-lined aisle should be dotted with blush rose petals to match the abundant arrangements that anchored each pew and were held by each bridesmaid. Right on cue, the signal from her business partner came through her earpiece, and Caroline gave a firm nod to her assistants to open the double wooden doors in unison for maximum effect before quickly ducking out of sight, knowing that the photographers would be poised with their cameras, eager to capture this moment. As the tearful bride became visible, a gasp went up from the friends and family who had all gathered in the candlelit stone church to witness this blissful occasion.

There. Job done. At least the emotionally challenging part. The real work would be at the reception, where Caroline was headed now. She walked quickly but lightly, knowing how heels could echo in these old buildings, and quietly pushed open the front door, going so far as to close it oh so slowly behind her, lest it slam. She may not like weddings, but she certainly didn't plan to ruin one, and definitely not when the bride's family was paying her enough to cover her rent for the next three months.

Enough to have made her take the job in the first place, and that was only because she'd had two cancelations in the past six months—one for a twenty-fifth-anniversary party that resulted in a divorce before they could even pick out a cake, and another for an engagement party when the proposal had ended in tears instead of a promise of forever.

Not that Caroline was surprised. Nope, not at all. Love was for the lucky few. And even then, she always had to wonder just how long it would last. Sometimes, over a glass of wine, she and Maya, her best-friend-turned-business-partner, even bet on it.

Take today's couple, who were probably joining hands at this very moment. Caroline gave them two years tops. More if they had kids early into the marriage, which she knew the bride hoped for—and the groom did not.

But none of this was her problem! The only thing that Caroline needed to worry about was making sure that the reception was ready by the time the guests arrived.

She looked at her clipboard and, with a click of her pen, checked off the items that were already completed or in motion. Bridesmaids accounted for and dressed. Flowers delivered. Limousines on time and in order of appearance. Check, check, check. Groom at the altar. Check.

In her experience, that was the biggest one, and even today, when it wasn't her wedding, she'd held her breath until one of her assistants had confirmed that the groom had, indeed, arrived at the church, and even then, she'd still felt a little funny until she was sure that he'd walked his mother down the aisle. Surely he wouldn't turn back after that. Even she wasn't that cynical.

Caroline opened her car door, letting the hot air release for a moment, and fanned herself with her clipboard as she waited for Maya to join her. Her friend appeared through the door a minute later, carefully closing it just as Caroline had, before all but sprinting down the stone steps, which was no small feat in four-inch heels.

"Start the engine!" Maya whisper-yelled as she hurried to the secondhand SUV that Caroline had purchased when she and her former college roommate started their event-planning company three years ago, after Caroline moved back to her college town.

Caroline slid into the driver's seat, started the engine, and blasted the air conditioning. Luckily for the bride and groom, it was a warm June day, and for more reasons than her aversion to weddings, she longed to kick off her heels, close her eyes, and imagine that she was dipping her bare toes in the cool ocean water where she usually spent her summers —and every other season to boot.

"That was beautiful!" Maya said breathlessly as she buckled her seat belt.

Caroline said nothing as she maneuvered the giant

vehicle with ample trunk space out of the parking lot and merged with the traffic.

It *was* a beautiful wedding: they'd seen to it themselves. But that didn't mean she was going to gush over it. Maya knew that she had agreed to this project only because they had a dip in revenue recently and nothing else on the calendar for the foreseeable future—something that was giving her night sweats. There was no excuse not to take the wedding, really, even though in the past, Caroline's refusal would have been excuse enough. They'd been scrambling since they first decided to open their event-planning company when Caroline moved back to Philly. It seemed that no matter how great their website, how many ads they took out, or how many business cards they handed out, their business relied nearly exclusively on opportunity. The problem with that was not every guest at a party they planned had intentions of throwing one of their own. Some couldn't afford their fees. Others had no occasions. Others, like the Dawsons, decided to call it quits rather than celebrate twenty-five years together.

Which brought them here, to this day, where they had, by Caroline's estimation, exactly forty-two minutes to get to the hotel, park, and make sure that all of the vendors were cooperating.

One of their assistants was already in place at the site of the reception, which was some relief, but only some. Becky was a new hire, much like the two assistants still at the church, because keeping staff wasn't exactly easy when the work wasn't consistent.

"I should have stayed at the hotel to greet the vendors," Maya said, muttering to herself.

"I'm sure Becky has it covered," Caroline assured her. "You were just there, what, half an hour ago? What could have gone wrong since then?"

But as soon as she said it, she felt her stomach knot with dread. A lot could go wrong with a wedding, and she was proof of that.

Five minutes later, she screeched to a halt outside of one of Philadelphia's most historic hotels, inches from a five-foot gilded planter that could have left a sizable dent in her hood. Maya's door was already partially open before she'd fully braked. Caroline could only shake her head as she watched her friend sprint past the doormen and through the revolving doors, where she'd been forced to slow her pace in the name of professionalism.

Caroline was nearly laughing by the time she'd pulled around the corner and into the adjacent parking garage. Leaving her friends and family in Cape Cod hadn't been painless, but having Maya by her side certainly made it easier. Even on days like this. They'd picked up right where they'd left off after college, both single, both happy to explore the city together. Most days, Caroline didn't even think about what she'd left behind.

Or who.

Keeping busy helped, too, and Caroline happily hurried to the staff entrance, where, even though she wasn't staff, she was granted entry. She passed through the kitchen, pleased to see that the appetizers they'd carefully selected were being taken out of ovens or plated. A three-tier wedding cake sat safely in the corner, waiting to be presented. Waiters in formal wear were pouring glasses of champagne and then setting them in the large glass-fronted refrigerator to chill before serving.

Satisfied, Caroline took the back hallways to the ballroom, which even she had to admit was, indeed, beautiful. The bride had chosen an assortment of roses for the arrangements, and each table was anchored with an oversize gilded vase filled with colorful flowers. Every place setting was accounted for, and the band was already tuning their instruments near the dance floor.

Caroline pushed through the French doors that led onto the stone patio, where Maya and Becky were adjusting some of the high-top tables. In the corner, a man in a tuxedo stood behind the full-service bar. Roses spilled from every surface.

"It's perfect," Caroline said, feeling satisfied. "Becky, why don't you make sure that all the appetizers are accounted for? The guests who aren't being photographed will arrive as soon as the ceremony ends and they'll be expecting food and drinks immediately."

Maya turned to her with large eyes once Becky had disappeared back inside.

Caroline felt an old familiar swell of panic rise in her chest. "What is it? What's wrong?"

Her mind replayed everything she'd just seen, cross-checking it with the list that was in her hands and fully memorized.

"Now's probably not the best time to tell you..." Maya looked like she might cry, and Caroline suddenly felt like she might, too.

She'd been feeling emotional all day, triggered by the mere thought of having to witness another bride fare better than she did. To be loved. Cherished. By the man who had promised to do just that.

And now Maya had bad news. As much as Caroline dreaded what she was about to hear, she also knew that she had no choice.

"We don't have much time—"

But Maya shook her head. "It's not about the event. Everything is in place. It's perfect, like you said. Which only makes what I'm about to say all the more difficult."

"What is it?" Caroline realized she had raised her voice when she caught the eye of the bartender. Handsome, she noted. Not that she was looking. No, she'd given up on love three years ago. It was the best thing she'd ever done other than open this business.

"I...took a new job," Maya said, wringing her hands.

"You *what*?" Caroline stared at her friend, trying to understand what she was saying. She'd taken a job. She was leaving their business. Leaving her...all on her own?

It wasn't the same as being jilted on the morning of her wedding, but somehow, right now, it felt very much the same. The future that she'd planned on was suddenly gone, and she was all alone. Again.

"You know that business has never been stable," Maya started to explain. "There are some months when we're worried about when the next client will come along."

"But then they do," Caroline replied.

"They do, but it's always a gamble, Caroline." Maya sighed. "I want security."

"Doesn't everyone?" Caroline said, and that little piece of her heart began to ache again. She thought she'd built her own security after leaving her hometown and all those bad memories behind. Now, she felt it slipping away.

"I need a guarantee," Maya pleaded.

Now Caroline barked out a laugh. "There's no such thing."

If there were, then the Dawsons would have toasted to twenty-five more years together. Then she would have just celebrated her third wedding anniversary with her childhood sweetheart.

Maya looked at her pityingly for a moment. "I took an in-house position. Event planner. Full-time work. Full benefits, too."

"Wait... Here?" Caroline looked around the hotel, one of the best in the city, remembering how Maya had always insisted on handling the meetings with the manager.

"I was surprised as you are when they offered me the job," Maya explained. "And...I couldn't turn it down."

"I understand," Caroline said after a beat. And she did. Business hadn't been steady—ever. Every month was a scramble. And no matter how successful their events were, when they were over, there was usually a lull before the next one. But then there was always that celebration when a new client did come along. One that they usually shared with a bottle of wine—admittedly a cheap one, but still. They were in it together.

She stared at her friend, seeing the hope in her eyes, the need for Caroline to forgive her.

How could she fault her best friend for choosing a sure

thing? She wanted the best for Maya, of course she did.

But she wanted the best for herself, too.

"I just need a moment before the guests arrive," Caroline said, inching backward to the door on shaking legs.

Maya nodded, knowing that she would need time to process this, and Caroline hurried through the ballroom, bypassing the nearest bathroom, to the doors that led to the pretty little garden that had been ruled too small to accommodate two hundred wedding guests. She dropped onto a bench and waited for the tears to spill, and then she quickly dabbed them away with one of the tissues she always carried with her, especially at events, because it was her job to be prepared for anything.

She just hadn't been prepared for this.

When the last of them had dried up, she pulled out her phone to check the time and saw that she had two missed calls from her sister Annie. They didn't speak often, mostly because they were both too busy with their careers, and not at all since Annie had moved back to Harmony Cove in April. Caroline hadn't taken it personally; she knew that a move was never easy and that Annie was preoccupied with taking over the family newspaper. Like Caroline, Annie had experienced her share of heartache. Only, unlike Caroline, she had recently united with her ex and that was, obviously, something that Caroline would not be doing now—not that she'd ever entertained such a thing. Not lately, at least.

In hindsight, however, she wondered if Annie had just been avoiding her. She wouldn't be the only one. Molly's texts had become less frequent in recent weeks and Val's interaction was briefer than ever. And then there was Hillary, who had faded away while Caroline was too busy trying to drum up business or make the most of the few events that she had that she had barely even noticed.

Or questioned it.

She tapped the screen and two rings later, Annie's familiar voice came on the line, bringing with it all the comfort that Caroline needed in this moment and had somehow pushed away over the years, along with the rest of her past.

"I don't have very long to talk," she told her sister. Duty called, especially given that from now on, all the events would fall squarely on her. That was if any more events presented themselves. As of tonight, she was officially unemployed. Again. Tomorrow she'd be starting over. Alone.

And despite having moved here three years ago to do just that—start over—she still hadn't found what she was looking for.

Maybe she'd never known what it was that she wanted.

"I'm afraid you're going to hang up on me anyway when you hear what I have to say," Annie said.

"I already know all about Hillary and *Tim's* wedding." Unless there was another surprise, this was the only invitation that she'd received—and promptly tossed in the trash. "Or should I say our cousin and the man I was supposed to marry?"

"It is pretty scandalous," Annie admitted with a sigh.

"I'm sure that Aunt Marcy is tickled pink," Caroline replied, knowing their father's sister's ways all too well. As the gossip columnist for the family's small-town newspaper, she lived for this type of story.

"I'll do my best to make sure she doesn't put her own spin on things," Annie said, knowing their aunt was prone to embellishment. "You do know that I'm the co-editor of the paper now, right?"

Caroline felt bad that she hadn't wished her sister congratulations yet, but planning today's event had kept her working around the clock these last few weeks—something she was grateful for, all things considered. And if she was being honest with herself, once word of the wedding had reached Caroline, she'd been dodging Annie probably as much as her sister had been avoiding her.

"Mom told me that you moved back from Seattle when I talked to her last month. Funny that she didn't mention Hillary's upcoming wedding."

Instead, she'd found out the old-fashioned way. It had been quite a shock, coming back to her apartment after a long day of cake and menu sampling, to find the creamy white envelope tucked inside her stash of bills. She was usually in charge of sending invitations, not receiving them. She'd seen the return address—her aunt Sandra, in Harmony Cove—and still thought nothing of it. Sandra owned a clothing boutique; perhaps she was having a fashion show. It wouldn't be the first one. And so she'd stood in the hallway of her small one-bedroom unit with a rent she could barely afford and popped the seal.

And yes, she had screamed.

"There's a lot that Mom probably didn't mention," Annie grumbled.

Caroline frowned, forgetting for a moment that she was equally mad at her sisters for failing to warn her about their cousin's engagement to her former fiancé. "What does that mean?"

Annie hesitated for a moment and then let out a long breath. "It's not my place to tell you this, but someone has to. Mom and Dad are...separated."

Caroline sat straight up in shock. Sure, she had become a little cynical when it came to love. Okay, more than a little, but who could blame her? The first and only man she had ever loved had stood her up on their wedding day. That would leave anyone questioning the endurance of love. But her parents? They had the kind of love that she never questioned. They were the high school sweethearts who had made it. Who had built not just a home, but businesses together. They'd raised four kids. They had date nights, even if they were just at home, on the back patio. They cuddled when they watched Christmas movies. They *held hands*.

She and Tim had never held hands. For a while after the breakup, she'd wondered if that had been a sign. But then she told herself that she didn't believe in signs. She didn't believe in anything, really.

But she believed in her parents. And she assumed that if and when she was ever ready to step foot on the Cape again, they'd be there, waiting. Together.

"What do you mean...separated?" she hedged.

"I mean that Dad moved out," Annie said matter-of-factly. Clearly, she'd had time to adjust to this news. "Or should I say, Mom kicked him out."

"*What*?" Caroline couldn't believe it. Not their mother. Not the mother who loved nothing more than making a nest for her family, feeding them nourishing meals with ingredients she grew in her garden, not getting worked up over little details like shoes being left where someone could trip or rooms being messy. She had her house, her children, her café, and her husband. And she was content. She always said as much. And it showed by the glow in her face. "That doesn't sound like something she would do."

Annie let out a strange little laugh. "Well, she's been doing a lot of stuff lately that is out of character."

"What does Dad say?" Caroline asked. Then, because she had so many questions, she blurted, "How long has this been going on?"

"Since September," Annie said.

"*September*?" Caroline clasped a hand over her mouth when she realized how loudly she'd spoken. She glanced around the garden. Still alone.

"I know. I only found out when I came back to town." Annie sighed.

Separated. Caroline couldn't make sense of this! She sat there absorbing this information. All these months and she'd never known. She had been busy, trying to build this failing business, trying to scrape by, to make something of this so-called new life. To prove that she could be happy, all on her own. That her future was still bright.

She hadn't been there when her family might have needed her most. And the fact that this was the first she was hearing of this...separation...filled her with shame.

"It turns out that Harmony Cove is a hotbed for drama," Annie said.

"Aunt Marcy must be having a field day," Caroline said miserably.

"Even Marcy knows that some things are too personal for idle gossip," Annie replied.

They fell silent for a moment while Caroline took in the news. There were so many things she wanted to know, and so many answers she feared.

"Where's Dad living?" she asked.

"Above the newspaper office," Annie said with a sigh. "I'm sure you heard about his retirement."

Caroline had, in that call with her mother. She'd called her father immediately afterward to congratulate him. Neither of them had breathed a word about their troubles.

"Anyway," Annie said. "I thought you should know."

Yes, she should know. She should have known months ago, long before her most recent talk with her mother where none of this was ever mentioned. She should have done something—anything.

"First Hillary and Tim and now this." Caroline shook her head, then looked up, around the garden. She'd become so engrossed in the call that she'd nearly forgotten where she was and where she needed to be.

But it wasn't at the wedding reception for her newly married clients. And it wasn't on the terrace to make sure that the guests had enough cocktail napkins. It wasn't back to her empty apartment or to her equally empty office, where she'd sit for hours trying to drum up new business.

It was in Harmony Cove. Cape Cod. With her three sisters. Her parents. Her family, however fractured it may be.

It was time to go home. At long last.

Even if the timing could not have been worse.

Two

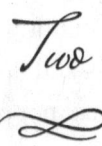

Lucas Reynolds felt like he was experiencing déjà vu. He stood with his arms out, legs slightly spread, getting his sleeve and hemline measured—for the second time in three years. Once again, as the older and only brother, he was playing the best man in Tim's wedding. And once again, he silently questioned his brother's ability to go all the way through with it.

He said nothing, instead taking a seat the first chance he had while Tim discussed the different color, tie, and vest options with the shop owner. Last time around, when Tim was planning to marry his high school sweetheart, Caroline Baker, Lucas had shown a little more interest, offering up his opinion when asked, going so far as to suggest a pocket square, even when he didn't exactly support the marriage. This time, he knew better and chose to conserve his energy for more important matters, like getting Tim to the ceremony. For the bride's sake, he hoped his brother did come through on his promise, but right now, he had other business to tend to.

He pulled out his phone and skimmed through his emails, hating to be away from the office for too long on a weekday. Only forty-five minutes had elapsed since he'd last checked—an hour tops—and in that time, half a dozen messages from investors had popped up—a daily occurrence since the hotel project he was overseeing had officially gotten approval from the town to break ground. He skimmed the latest from contractors on the status of various permits, one from the designer with yet another new design for the lobby, and three résumés from mediocre chefs vying for the job of head chef of what would be the hotel's signature restaurant when it opened (knock wood) next spring. Lucas flagged a few of the emails to review later, deleted the ones from the chefs, and heaved a heavy sigh.

Wallace Hadley was requesting a meeting tomorrow. He was their biggest investor, one that Lucas had secured himself, while Tim had wined and dined the rest in the initial meetings, the only part of his job at the family development firm that he took real interest in or enjoyed.

But Wallace was old-school. More Lucas's speed. He was buttoned-up, professional to what Tim would call a fault, and he was cautious. He also lived in Boston and had no real reason for a last-minute social visit to the Cape.

Lucas's palms felt sweaty when he stuffed the phone back into his pocket, out of sight. But not, unfortunately, out of mind.

"How's the project coming along?" Tim asked from the podium where he was now trying on a navy suit. It was more relaxed than the black tux he'd chosen for his first wedding attempt, but then, he and Hillary were planning a beach wedding rather than a formal affair.

Planning was the operative word. There were plans the last time, too, mostly set in place by the then-bride, of all people, the current bride's cousin. Plans that Tim couldn't see through to the finish, leaving Lucas to be the one to step up and break the bad news.

His jaw set when he thought of the position he'd been left in that day, how Caroline's pretty face had clouded with confusion as he explained that Tim wouldn't be coming to the church after all, how he'd watched a hundred different emotions pass through her eyes while she said nothing at all. That was the part that still haunted him. She'd just stood there, searching for answers he couldn't give, staring at him, as if he had any power to change things.

Shifting back to Tim's question, Lucas cleared his throat, more than happy to talk about his plans for their family business's newest and biggest project at the edge of town. Unlike Tim, when Lucas made plans, he saw them through to the end, even when things got tough, and even when, like lately, they felt downright impossible.

The hotel hadn't come together as easily as he'd hoped, first with pushback from some members of town worrying a hotel of this size would disrupt the tranquility, but he'd be damned if he'd give up now, and that wasn't because he had investors breathing down his neck. He'd waited his entire life for a project just like this to come along—not just because it brought him back to Harmony Cove for good, but because it was something he could care about and get behind. Eventually, the town had, too, especially the small shop owners who depended on tourist revenue and felt its absence in the cold winter months when the only people visiting the Cape were family for the holidays.

In the end, the plan was passed, and they'd broken ground last month. When it was finished, it would be a thing of beauty. A worthy addition to his hometown. Something to be proud of.

For the community.

And for himself.

Lucas bit back a sarcastic response to his brother's question. If Tim would show up at the office more often, he might not need to ask. Of course, Tim had no trouble making an appearance at the golf course under the guise of doing business.

But he didn't feel like arguing today, not when he was worried about the wedding and now the meeting with Wallace tomorrow.

"We're on schedule. If we keep going like this, then we should be open in less than a year," Lucas said, knowing that this was ambitious because things came up with a project as big as this one, they always did, but taking any more time would push them off into the next tourist season, which was at its peak during the summer months here on the Cape.

It was pitched as an all-American family resort. A nod to simpler times. There would be lawn games, a formal dinner, and dancing afterward, with a live band that would play Thursday through Saturday, every week of May through August. Bikes could be rented for the day, and tents for the beach, too. There would be an ice cream parlor on-site, and a high-end restaurant, too. It would be a place that families would return to, year after year. It would be a place filled with wholesome traditions, one where screentime was abandoned for some good old-fashioned fun.

He had investors counting on him. And he hadn't spent the past year trying to rebrand his father's company just to admit defeat now. He'd taken a development firm known for putting the bottom line above everything—and anyone—else, and promised his investors a better experience, one built on family values that he alone seemed determined to uphold. He gave his employees a generous family leave package, more time off for holidays and sick days, and he brought back the annual holiday party, something his father saw no point in spending money on if it didn't pad his wallet as a result. The wholesome image of the new hotel wasn't just his chance to prove that he had reshaped the company, it was also the only thing keeping the business going right now. With so many people working from home in recent years, office properties had taken a hit, and it had been Lucas's idea to shift Reynolds Properties into hotel development. He'd seen an opportunity the moment an old estate that had consumed the huge lot along the bay came available, putting up most of his life's savings to show he was serious. He'd taken a risk. A big one. And now he had to make sure that it paid off.

"Too bad the new hotel wasn't open this year," Tim mused. "Would have been a nice spot for the wedding."

"You're fine with a beach wedding, though," Lucas said.

It was, as Tim had said more than once, "casual." Casual suited Tim. In business, where he preferred to bring in new investors on the golf course or the nearest and most expensive watering hole, and, it would seem, in romance.

"Do you have the guest list finalized?" Lucas asked carefully because he was well aware that as a member of the bride's family, Caroline had been invited. He'd been holding off asking Tim, knowing that the topic of Caroline was sensitive, that his silence on the subject spoke more than any words ever could.

Would she really come? Lucas couldn't imagine she would want to, and he hoped that she wouldn't, for Tim's sake. Tim had never tried to make things right with her, and, after playing the field for a few years, he was now engaged to Caroline's cousin of all people, but there was always a chance, always a possibility, that if he saw Caroline again, the feelings that he'd suppressed would resurface and then...

And then.

Lucas couldn't even think about it.

"Dad isn't coming." Tim tossed him a look that betrayed his disapproval. It wasn't often that Tim showed any emotion, especially when it came to their parents, and a familiar feeling crept up in Lucas's chest. "He said he already had a trip planned and it was short notice."

It was short notice, not that Lucas was going to point that out. He didn't need to plant any doubts in Tim's mind.

"If it hadn't been this excuse, he probably would have found another," Tim grumbled.

Again, Lucas said nothing, even though it was true. Their father hadn't been the most reliable parent since divorcing their mother, and he certainly wasn't the most sentimental.

"For the best," he said gruffly, and Tim nodded his agreement. "He'd only end up arguing with Mom about something and sour the day."

Whether or not this would be the case, he didn't know, but he watched Tim's expression until he was convinced that his brother wasn't upset by this news.

"Anything else worth noting?" he asked, trying to sound casual.

"Hillary's taking care of all the wedding details," Tim said, seeming disinterested, just as he had the last time.

A funny feeling churned in his stomach, and Lucas did his best to push it back. A lot of men he knew left the wedding planning to their fiancées. If he ever got married, he'd probably do the same.

Not that he would ever get married. He'd seen what marriage did to people, brought out the worst in them, like his parents, both times around, until they'd both settled into singlehood, his father dating women younger and younger with each passing year.

And then, of course, there was Tim, who couldn't even make it to the altar last time around.

Lucas sat back in his chair, thinking rationally. Caroline hadn't been spotted in Harmony Cove since the week following her wedding day. He could only assume that for all the reasons cited, Caroline wouldn't be attending the wedding, which was for the best for everyone.

"So you haven't seen the final guest list," Lucas clarified, needing to know, wishing that there was some way he could know, to be prepared.

"You know how excited Hillary's mom is about this wedding," Tim remarked. "They have it all covered."

Lucas frowned at him. The wedding was in ten days. It had been a short engagement compared to the long one he'd had with Caroline. That didn't make Lucas feel any better. Impulsivity led only to problems, in his experience. But then, he was the type who liked to set a plan in motion and think out all the steps before taking action.

And he and Tim couldn't be more different.

Sandra Ross seemed like the type of woman who would love to oversee the details of her eldest daughter's wedding—and the first of her three daughters'. She was a social butterfly; a divorcée, she enjoyed the town's lively nightlife, especially during the summer season, when day-trippers and tourists flocked to the Cape. She lived for a big crowd and a good party, and she loved dressing up for an occasion, too. Lucas couldn't remember the last time he hadn't seen her in full glam, even when he was collecting his morning coffee at the Sweet Harmony Café.

"Sandra's been working night and day on this wedding," Tim said. "She's been personally sewing all of the bridesmaid dresses and the wedding dress."

Hm. And on a very tight timeline. Tim had proposed only two months ago. And he and Hillary had dated for only four months before that.

Yet here they were, the Reynolds brothers, preparing for the day when Tim would commit to Hillary for life. He couldn't do it with Caroline, despite dating her since they were kids. And their parents certainly couldn't do it.

It was like a curse, Lucas always thought. No one in their

family could make love last, and that was why he didn't bother even trying. He had other passions to make life interesting, and right now the hotel was his top priority.

But making sure that Tim went through with this wedding and that he didn't let another woman down was important, too. It wouldn't look good for the Reynolds name. And it certainly wouldn't look good for business.

And Lucas was willing to do whatever it took to make that happen. To break the family cycle once and for all.

Caroline woke up in her childhood bed and stared out the window at the blue sky, hidden only by the leaves of the tree branches, trying not to remember one of the last days that she'd opened her eyes to the very same view. The anniversary of that awful day had come and gone two weeks ago—she supposed Tim and Hillary weren't that callous, if either of them had even remembered the date.

She pushed the soft and worn patchwork quilt off her legs and hopped out of bed before she started second-guessing her decision to come back to Harmony Cove even more than she already did.

The house was quiet, so different from the days of her childhood when all four Baker girls were banging closet doors and arguing over who could shower first. Annie had moved back into her old apartment, now sharing it with Val, who had taken over the lease when Annie moved away, and one check of her watch confirmed that it was late, nearly eleven, meaning that her mother and her youngest sister,

Molly, who lived out back in the carriage house, would have been at the Sweet Harmony Café for hours by now, and that Caroline's sleeping pill had certainly done its job.

She'd gotten in late. Her flight had been delayed. And while both Annie and Valerie had offered to pick her up at the ferry in Provincetown, Caroline needed some time to settle in and opted instead for a taxi. The truth was that she needed a moment to collect herself, to accept the fact that she was back in her hometown, after three years away, and to process how she felt about that.

She'd been so embarrassed when she'd left. So ashamed that her heartache had been on public display for the entire town to witness and whisper about—and the longer she'd stayed away, the more she'd wondered what kind of gossip her return would stir up.

Leave it to her to choose this timing. Only now, maybe people's attention would be on Tim.

And Hillary.

Caroline's heart hurt when she thought of her cousin. Her sweet, funny, beautiful cousin marrying that...that...

Nope. Not going there. She wasn't going back to the past. She wasn't going to spend her time here ruminating over feelings that she had worked hard to put to rest. She was here for her parents. Nothing more.

And seeing as she'd been too worn out last night to get into things with her mother, she had no excuse but to have a conversation today.

Feeling restless, Caroline put on one of her best summery outfits in case she ran into Tim—or even Hillary for that matter—and walked into town, deciding that she couldn't avoid it forever any more than she could delay having a heart-to-heart with her mother.

She began slowly, her eyes darting this way and that, until she shook off her paranoia and laughed at herself. Her childhood street was surrounded by the same cedar-shingled homes owned by the same friendly families that she'd known all her life. The Reynoldses lived in a big house on the other side of Harmony Cove, one of the few lucky ones to own property facing the Atlantic. Maybe Tim was living at Hillary's apartment in town, or maybe he had bought something of his own when he moved back. She didn't know.

And she didn't care.

Instead, she focused on the beautiful homes, the flowers that were starting to bloom, the bright pink roses and the peonies that were so fragrant, poking out of the whitewashed picket fences. When she finally approached town and the bay came into view, she held her breath for a moment, letting herself take it in, committing it to heart, even though she knew that it had been there all this time.

Just like a part of her had been here. Home.

The sky was a deep blue, not a cloud in sight, and the air was salty and warm, with the slightest hint of a breeze. Feeling relaxed in a way that she only ever could near the water, Caroline gathered up her confidence and blended in with the crowds that walked along the sidewalk, mostly locals, some of whom gave her a double look and then a smile, hurrying her pace now toward the café, where she knew that she was bound to see more familiar faces because Sweet Harmony wasn't just a place for great food.

It was a place for great company.

"Hey!" a voice called out from somewhere down the block. "Caroline! Caroline!"

Caroline's heart started to pound, even though the voice was female, and she looked across the street to see her sister Valerie holding on to two dog leashes with one hand and waving to her with the other.

Her troubles were momentarily forgotten as she watched the big golden retrievers all but drag her sister across the street. Val jogged, struggling to keep up with them.

"They're excited," Val explained, out of breath.

"I'm excited," Caroline said, reaching out to hug her freckle-faced sister. Val was the second to the youngest, with Molly being the baby, but Caroline felt protective of their entire little flock. "I've missed you."

Saying it, and seeing her sister, with her wild dark hair and bright green eyes, she couldn't have meant it more.

Her heart ached for the time lost. For the reason why she'd left.

For why she'd felt the need to stay away.

"I can see that not much has changed since I've been away." Caroline laughed and bent to give the friendly dog nearest a scratch behind the ears.

Val, however, gave her a knowing look. "I know why you're back. You heard about Mom and Dad."

"And Hillary and Tim." Caroline raised an eyebrow.

"Hey, can you blame us?" Val quipped. "None of us wanted to be the bearer of *that* news. None of us even want it to be happening."

So she wasn't alone in that sentiment. But then, her sisters always had her back.

And once, Hillary did, too.

"So," Caroline said, getting back to the biggest problem, and one that she might be able to help. "What is going on with Mom and Dad? I got in late last night and it didn't seem like the right time to talk to her. You know how Mom and Molly always turn in early because they have to get up before sunrise to be at the café. I didn't even see Molly last night. She had a headache and promised to see me today."

"I think you should talk to Mom directly," Valerie said. "And as for Molly, you know she was dodging you, right?"

Caroline frowned for a moment and then grinned. Molly would have wanted to stay out of the fray until the conflict was resolved. And given that Caroline was back in town after three years because her parents were separated and it happened to coincide with her ex's wedding, she supposed that this was more stress than Molly could handle.

Heck, it was more stress than she could handle.

But she was here. And looking into her sister's familiar face, feeling the ocean air whip through her hair, she was glad she was. For the moment, at least.

"I'm heading over to the café now," Caroline told Val. "Want to join me?"

Valerie shook her head. "I have to get these two home before my next client has an accident on the white sofa again. He's a leg lifter, that one, and he doesn't like to be kept waiting."

They shared a laugh and a hug, and then Val was gone, trotting behind the giant dogs, leaving Caroline alone to deal with her mother, because her sister was right—Molly probably wouldn't be much of a buffer when it came to this conversation.

The family business was hardly the place to unload their dirty laundry, but seeing as Sharon Baker spent more time at the café than she did at home, it might be the best place to sit down and understand just why someone would throw away thirty-five years of marriage.

Maybe, just maybe, it would shed a little light on how someone could throw away a twelve-year relationship and a plan for a future together.

Caroline felt more relaxed when she opened the door to Sweet Harmony, knowing that there was no chance of running into Tim here. He may be shameless enough to date and then propose to her cousin, but he knew better when it came to Caroline's mother and sister. The Bakers were a tight-knit family—or at least, they had been, until the matriarch decided to kick their father to the curb.

Caroline bypassed the counter, where a college-aged girl was taking to-go orders—the addition of the seasonal staff was always the first mark of the start of the summer, meaning the tourists wouldn't be far behind—and pushed through the swinging door into the kitchen. Her mom and Molly were standing side by side at the big center island, one chopping vegetables and the other mixing a vinaigrette. They both stopped when the door creaked, signaling her arrival.

But it was Caroline who froze.

"Mom?" She stared at the woman who made a mission of living life practically. Jeans, a good cotton T-shirt or warm wool sweater on a chilly day, gray streaked hair pulled back into a bun while she worked.

Instead, she saw a woman with her mother's face who had decidedly pink highlights.

"It's been too long, darling!" Sharon said as she came around the island, arms outstretched.

Clearly.

Last summer, when her parents had visited her in Philadelphia, her mother had still looked like her usual self.

And she'd still been blissfully married to Caroline's father, too.

Only now, Caroline wondered if they were ever as content as they'd seemed. She didn't know up from down anymore. She couldn't trust her own judgment.

Caroline searched her sister's face for an explanation as she leaned in to hug her mother, who at least felt the same, even if she didn't look the same. When it was Molly's turn, Caroline hissed into her ear, "What's up with the hair?"

Molly just giggled nervously and quickly went back to her task of chopping tomatoes, skirting the question.

"I can't believe you're here," Sharon said, her eyes roaming over Caroline's face, much the way Caroline's were no doubt roaming over hers. "I have to say, I couldn't have been more surprised when you said that you were coming back for the wedding."

"Oh, I'm not here for the wedding," Caroline was quick to say.

Her mother frowned. "But the visit. After all these years. Now, of all times? What other reason could you possibly have?"

Caroline caught Molly's eye but said nothing. It wasn't

the time, not when her family members were clearly hard at work and the café was full of hungry customers.

"This is a big step," Sharon went on. "We all know this must be so difficult for you, but the fact that you've found the courage to come here and support your cousin just proves how far you've come."

Caroline stared at her mother, for more reasons than one. Was that...lip gloss? Since when did her mother wear more than ChapStick?

"I came back for a *visit*, not for the wedding." Caroline hadn't realized this wasn't clear. She hadn't exactly replied to the wedding invitation. How could she, when it was already buried deep in the trash, and, maybe, torn into a dozen pieces?

Now her mother looked stricken as she glanced at Molly, whose earlier concern turned to one of alarm.

"Oh, but...I thought..." Her mother wrung her hands. "And I told Sandra..."

"You thought I was okay with my ex-fiancé marrying my cousin?" Caroline looked quizzically at the woman who usually understood her so well.

"It's just that you've never visited since you left, and you and Hillary were always so close, and with the wedding being next week..." Her mother trailed off and looked desperately at Molly, whom Caroline knew was too tactful to push the subject. "I hoped this meant you were finally over what happened."

"I am over it," Caroline said, even though she wasn't so sure that she would ever be. Who actually got over the only man they'd ever loved disappearing on the morning of their wedding, only to resurface years later engaged to another member of the family? "It's not like I'm still hung up on a man who couldn't be bothered to show up to our wedding."

Because that would be pathetic, even if it was half-true. What she was still hung up on was the burn of embarrassment she'd felt when she'd had to duck out the back door of the church, the gasps and whispers from the guests chasing her all the way to the duck pond, where she'd dirtied the skirt of her beautiful satin gown on the path. What she was still hung up on was the fact that Tim hadn't even had the courage to break things off himself, but that his brother had done it for him. What still stung was that Tim had promised to love her forever, and without her even noticing, he'd just stopped.

And now he loved someone else. Enough to marry her.

And the fact that this someone was her cousin? Well, yes, she was rather hung up on that.

"Well, good, good!" her mother gushed. "Because you see…because I thought…"

Molly looked nervously at their mother. "You'd better just tell her, Mom."

"Tell me what?" Caroline demanded, her alarm rising. What more could there be? Her ex-fiancé was marrying her cousin, her parents were separated, and her mother had pink hair.

"It's just that Hillary's friend from college had a family emergency and she can't make it to the wedding after all. She was supposed to be a bridesmaid." Her mother looked at her pointedly.

Caroline shrugged but she didn't like the look in her

mother's eyes or the way Molly was now edging toward the kitchen door.

"They need to balance out the ladies and the gents," Sharon went on, her gaze beseeching. "And so, when I told Sandra that you were coming home, well, it just made perfect sense for you to...take that place."

Molly took that time to announce that she was going to check on the customers.

Caroline watched her sister disappear through the swinging door, wanting nothing more than to run after her. And straight out of town.

Instead, she took a few measured breaths and stared at her mother, trying to make the blood stop rushing in her ears.

"You told Sandra that I'd be a bridesmaid?" she repeated. "In *Tim's* wedding?"

Her mother nodded. "Oh, honey, it meant so much to Hillary to have your blessing!"

"My *blessing*?" Caroline echoed. "More like my pity. Good luck to her. We'll see if this wedding even happens."

"You don't think it's possible, is it?" Her mother's eyes went wide.

"Yes, Mom, I think it is more than possible for Tim to pull a runner like he did last time," Caroline said. Because for her to think otherwise, to believe that Tim was going to show up on the big day and stand at the altar, watching with love in his eyes as Hillary walked down the aisle, could only mean that he loved Hillary more than he'd ever loved her, and that...that didn't make any sense.

"I'm sure that thought is on a lot of people's minds," her

mother agreed sadly. "For Hillary's sake, I hope that doesn't happen. Even if I do think she could have done better. You know how I feel about that guy." Her gaze narrowed.

Now Caroline felt a smile tug at her mouth. She couldn't be mad at her mother—not when she'd always had her back.

"Why didn't you tell me about the wedding, Mom?" she asked gently, dropping onto one of the stools her mother used when her legs grew tired after a long day. *Why didn't you tell me a lot of things?* she wanted to say. "I had to find out through the invitation."

Her mother dragged another stool closer to hers before sitting. "To be honest, honey, I didn't want to hurt you. But when I heard you were coming back, I felt like I could finally stop worrying about you. I thought that you'd put that awful time in your life behind you, once and for all."

"I did, Mom," Caroline reassured her. More like she was trying to. She'd come this far, being back in Harmony Cove, and that had clearly sent a message. And refusing to be a bridesmaid would send a message, too. One that said she wasn't over what Tim did to her. Or maybe that she wasn't even over Tim at all.

With a heavy sigh, she said, "Fine. I'll fill in as a bridesmaid."

"You will?" Her mother leaned forward and hugged her so tight that Caroline could barely breathe. "Oh, honey, this will be for the best. You'll see! You'll go, you'll dance. Maybe you'll even meet someone new."

Caroline highly doubted that—not only because this was Harmony Cove, where she'd known everyone since she was old enough to toddle in the sand, but because she didn't want to meet anyone new. She was perfectly fine on her own.

Well, almost fine. And definitely better off on her own. At least she didn't have to worry about anyone letting her down or breaking her heart again.

Caroline dipped her chin and then gave a stern shake of her head. "I'm only doing this for you, Mom."

It was the entire reason she was here.

She hesitated, wanting to bring up her father, the separation, to ask what had brought all this on, including the pink hair and shiny lips, but her mother was hurrying back to the worktop now, rambling about the lunch crowd, and Caroline knew that now was not the time.

"I'm going to grab something to eat," she told her mother instead, hoping that she'd have her chance for a long and proper chat sooner than later.

"I put your favorite on the menu!" Sharon beamed. "In honor of your return."

"Shrimp rolls?" Caroline perked up a little at the promise of her mother's cooking.

With at least one thing to look forward to, she walked back into the café, and, spotting a rare empty table on the front patio, hurried to grab it. She was just about to triumphantly set her handbag on a rattan chair when a hand reached out and claimed it.

She looked up, bracing for one of those polite arguments people tended to have in situations like this, but all chance of this being a civil exchange halted when she realized she was staring into the dark eyes of none other than Lucas Reynolds.

"Caroline." Surprise registered on his face, and he seemed to step back, dropping his hand.

She couldn't bring herself to greet him in return. She couldn't bring herself to say anything to him, just like that awful day. And what could she have said, then or now? *Oh, thanks for letting me know that my fiancé won't be showing up for the wedding we only discussed every day for two years.* Or, *Hey, so good to see you again, hope you have better news today than the last time I saw you.*

She dropped onto the chair before he could stop her. The least he could do for her was let her have the table. It was her family's restaurant, after all. He had some nerve even showing up here at all.

"I didn't realize you were back in town," Lucas continued, showing no signs of leaving. His stare was unwavering, and he didn't seem to blink for several seconds.

Caroline forced herself to look at him properly, even though it pained her to do so, stirring up all the emotions from the last time she'd seen him. She and Lucas had never been close. He was four years older than Tim, meaning that they'd never hung out in the same social circle as kids, and he was always bossing Tim around, rolling his eyes if she and Tim laughed too hard while he was studying, or telling Tim that he had to drop her off an hour before her curfew so he could get a good night's rest.

Unlike Lucas, Tim was a good-time guy, the life of the party. A charmer. He had a way of making anyone he talked to feel like the most important person in the room with his hundred-watt smile and his shiny eyes that never seemed to stray.

He'd made her feel really special for long enough for her to be blind to his faults.

But she'd always been aware of Lucas's shortcomings, which were on full display. He was grumpy, uptight, the last person you'd want at a party. Maybe a better guest for a funeral.

Or the death of an engagement.

Now she saw that he didn't seem much older than her at all. His hairstyle had changed slightly since her wedding day, and the tousled look flattered him, as did the more casual clothing that he wore—his usual starched jeans swapped out for khaki pants, and his rigid button-down replaced with a linen shirt rolled to the elbows. But the bewilderment on his face was still there, pinching his eyebrows, pulling his full mouth into a frown.

He'd never been a fan of hers, and clearly, he still wasn't.

"If you're worried that I'm here to crash the wedding, you can rest assured," she told him cooly. "I was invited, seeing as I'm family."

"I didn't mean that," he stammered, but she didn't really care what he meant. She'd rather focus on what he'd done, and that was to callously walk into the bridal chamber, where she'd been waiting with her father and sisters for their cue to begin the procession, march straight up to her, and without bothering to mince words told her quickly and firmly that Tim wouldn't be coming and that he longer planned to marry her.

Talk about ripping off the Band-Aid. A little Novocain might have been nice.

"Actually, I've just learned that I won't only be attending

the wedding, but I'll also be participating in it." She managed to laugh at the irony of that. "I guess the only way I was ever going to be in a wedding with Tim was to be a bridesmaid instead of the bride."

Lucas looked pained. "Caroline."

She shook her head, wishing she hadn't let herself broach the topic. Her heart stung even more than her words, she was sure, which were wasted on a man like Lucas. Or on any Reynolds. They were a cold and heartless bunch, and her biggest mistake had been thinking that one of them could be different.

"You can tell your brother about the change in plans if he isn't already aware. I know how good you are at delivering messages," she added with a tight smile.

Lucas's mouth thinned as his eyes flashed. Point taken. Well, good.

She waited to see if he would say anything more, but instead, he backed away, said a quiet goodbye, and left her to enjoy the table, the warm sunshine, and a memory that she'd tried so hard to forget and now had never been clearer.

Three

The next afternoon, Caroline stood with Valerie and Molly outside their aunt Sandra's clothing shop, wondering again why she had agreed to not only attend but be a bridesmaid if she couldn't stop darting her eyes all over Water Street, bracing herself for a run-in with Tim.

Since seeing Lucas yesterday, she'd retreated to the comfort of her childhood house, where she'd mulled over family photos, sat on the porch with a glass of homemade lemonade, and feasted on the endless options stored in the fridge, each of her mother's recipes more delicious than the next, all while trying not to worry too much about her business—or lack thereof.

And of course, trying not to worry about her parents, who, like Molly, seemed to be dodging her. Her mother had been busy with her book club last night and her father had longstanding plans with a friend but promised to meet her for lunch today.

Caroline was too anxious about seeing Hillary to take

offense. Truth be told, she was a little relieved to have a chance to settle in and absorb all the news before having a heart-to-heart with her parents.

"Tell me that the dresses are at least pretty," Caroline pleaded to her sisters.

Valerie gave a little snort. "The dresses are at least pretty."

"You're just repeating what I said!" Caroline couldn't help but grin. Val might be in her late twenties by now, but she hadn't changed much over the years.

If only everything else could have stayed the same, Caroline thought, looking down the street at the church where she had once stood excitedly in a wedding gown, and beyond it, to the newspaper offices, where her father no longer worked but lived in the small apartment on the top floor.

It shouldn't have turned out this way. Her father should be at home, or at the café, her mother not far out of reach, passing each other those secret smiles that used to make Caroline and her sisters roll their eyes when they were teenagers and painfully aware of their parents' public displays of affection.

Now she longed to see her father swoop her mother into his arms and plant a kiss on her mouth in public.

Just like she longed to be the girl she once was—so full of hope. So certain that her life was going to turn out exactly as she'd thought it would.

Val shrugged. "I'm just telling you what you want to hear."

Molly winced. "The dresses aren't *terrible*. They have spaghetti straps, an A-line skirt—"

"And they're turquoise," Val said bluntly. She gave Molly

a hard look and then turned back to Caroline. "They'll at least look good with your eyes. And Annie's."

Caroline and Annie had both been blessed with their father's blue eyes, while Valerie and Molly had inherited their mother's green shade.

"Speaking of Annie, isn't she coming?" The event planner in Caroline couldn't help but make sure that the entire wedding party was accounted for at this final fitting. And she was still waiting for a moment to reunite with her next closest sister. Their plans to catch up last night had been thwarted when Sean's mother's health slipped. Caroline was only vaguely aware of how ill Mrs. Morrison was and grew concerned.

"She said she'd meet us here," Molly replied. "Deadlines and all."

Of course. Annie was running the newspaper now, meaning she was gainfully employed and had somewhere to be, things to do, on weekdays, and, given her job description, most weekends, too. Molly was only here on break before she went back to the café, and Valerie was in between walks for her dozens of canine clients.

And Caroline didn't know when the next event would come along for her to plan. She knew only that this time, she'd be doing it all on her own.

The thought was dreary enough to make her search for a distraction. "I guess we may as well go in. I can't hide forever."

Even though that's exactly what she'd tried to do for the past three years.

Aunt Sandra and her three daughters were inside the

boutique when Caroline stepped through the door, flanked by Valerie and Molly. Her aunt and cousins had been chatting excitedly before Caroline entered, but now they stopped and froze, and for a moment, Caroline wondered if they even knew she was coming, but then Hillary clasped her hands together and ran to her the best she could through the racks of clothes and accessories, which filled the space in a charmingly cluttered way.

"Caroline!" Hillary stopped just short of hugging her, but then, after a pause, did it anyway.

Caroline felt the pull of her cousin, who, being the same age, had been her best friend growing up, as close as any of her sisters, and at times, even closer. With their fair hair, some people even remarked that they could be sisters, which they secretly always longed to be. It was Hillary who stood beside Caroline on "twin day" at school, who sat with her every day at lunch, and who had been in the room that awful day when Lucas came in to make his brief and stilted announcement. She'd witnessed Caroline's devastation firsthand, shared in the heartbreak, and even brought over a big chocolate cake from their aunt Kathy's bakery the next day, which they'd eaten straight out of the box in Caroline's childhood bed since it wasn't like she was going back to the place she shared with Tim.

Hillary had shared in the pain of that experience, right down to the stomachaches from devouring every last bite of that two-tiered double-chocolate dessert.

Had Hillary forgotten that day, and the days that followed, or the months and years that took Caroline away from her and this town?

Caroline stared at Hillary and felt a hundred emotions rise up in her chest. There was love, of course, a fondness that couldn't be forgotten no matter how many years had passed since they'd last seen each other or how many months it had been since they'd last spoken. But there was hurt, too, reminding her of all that hadn't been shared, even when they'd once promised to never keep secrets. Even when they'd promised to always be on each other's side.

And there was just the simple comfort of being in Hillary's presence again. Reunited with the one person who knew her best, better than even her own sisters, the real twins. She saw the joy in Hillary's face, the way her eyes shone a little brighter than usual. And as much as it killed Caroline to even think about it, she knew that Hillary would make a beautiful bride.

"I can't tell you what it means to me that you're here," Hillary said, taking both of Caroline's hands in hers and squeezing them. "I didn't know if I should send an invitation, but it felt so wrong not to, and I couldn't imagine my wedding day without you, Caroline."

Oof. Pile on the guilt a little more. Caroline struggled to remain upset with Hillary as her cousin continued to talk about all their childhood memories, the good old days, the bond they shared, that in many ways she was more like a sister than her actual sisters, which sparked a cough from her mother.

"When I found out that you were coming..." Tears filled Hillary's eyes, making them turn as blue as the deepest part of the ocean on a clear summer day. "It's just like we always dreamed, Caroline. You and me, being bridesmaids in each other's weddings."

Caroline heard Valerie snort behind her, louder this time, and she stared at her cousin, unable to speak. Sure, they'd talked about that when they were little girls, but they'd left out the part about marrying the same guy—or one of them getting stood up at the altar.

Caroline was going to point out that she'd never gotten all the way to her wedding but then decided that she didn't have the energy to rehash it. They'd both moved on—one more than the other—and now Hillary was getting married. And Caroline was trying to support her.

Or at least fake it until the reception, at which point she imagined she'd slip away and have a good cry, and then hightail it out of town, this time never to return again.

"Maid of honor, actually," Caroline said, reminding Hillary of the part she'd played on that fateful day.

But Hillary's mouth just curved into a hopeful smile. "Exactly."

Uh-oh. Oh, no. Caroline's mother hadn't said anything of this sort. She darted a glance at Molly, whose eyes looked like they were about to pop.

"I know we've lost touch recently," Hillary started. "But...it wouldn't feel like my wedding day without you by my side. So...will you, Caroline? Be my maid of honor?"

Caroline became aware that she was breathing hard and that the entire room had fallen silent as everyone waited for her response. Feeling a little faint, she managed a nod, because she was unable to find the words required in this moment.

"Let me show you the dresses!" Hillary said, taking Caroline's hand and leading her to the back of the store where, sure enough, twelve turquoise dresses hung from a dress rack.

"It's a beach wedding," Hillary explained when Caroline didn't immediately say anything.

Caroline hadn't even had a chance to greet her other cousins or aunt, and now she took a moment to do just that, commenting as she did on how great the twins, Phoebe and Kayla, looked, how her aunt had never looked younger, which was true, and likely with the help of injectables, and how happy she was to see them all. Because she was. She'd missed them, even though she hadn't allowed herself to do that. Now, being surrounded by all these women who did, admittedly, feel like sisters, she had a deep sense of how empty her life had been without them all these years.

And how much emptier it would be now that she wouldn't be sharing her business or her days with Maya anymore.

She'd be completely on her own. In every possible way.

"How is life in Philly?" Aunt Sandra asked eagerly. "You must be so busy, running your own event-planning business!"

Everyone stared at Caroline, expecting her to confirm this.

With a weak nod, she did.

"All the more reason to be so happy that you found time to come home for this special occasion!" Aunt Sandra beamed.

Special occasion was one way to put it, Caroline thought

but did her best to smile and nod along, finding it was easier than speaking.

"Kathy's girls have already been through for their final fittings," Sandra announced. "Of course, I had to do Paige's dress from measurements alone since she's too busy in Boston to get back to town before the big day." She let out a steadying breath that showed her nerves and ushered the younger four women into dressing rooms, but Hillary held Caroline back for a moment.

Her eyes turned round with worry. "Are you sure...it's okay, Caroline?" she whispered urgently.

Up until this moment, Caroline had not felt that any of this was okay, but standing here, her hand clasped in her cousin's, her sisters and cousins just a few feet away, she knew that it would have to be. That love didn't make sense. That just like it wasn't her fault that Tim stopped loving her, it wasn't any more Hillary's fault that he did love her.

That for reasons she was yet to understand, some people made it and some people, however surprising or expected, didn't.

"Because if it's not okay, then I won't go through with it," Hillary said, staring at her.

Startled, Caroline blinked and then frowned. "What? No. No! I don't want you to do that."

And she realized in that moment that she didn't. What she wanted up until today was for Tim to have never dated Hillary, and certainly never to have proposed. What she wanted, really, was for Tim to live a sad, lonely life in which he regretted throwing away their relationship and breaking her heart up until his dying breath.

But she didn't want Hillary to call off her wedding when it was already planned. And she definitely didn't want her to call it off on account of her.

She wanted her cousin to be happy. She just struggled to believe that Tim Reynolds could be the man to make her so.

Taking a big breath, she forced herself to smile and say, "Tell me all about what you have planned for the big day."

This was in her wheelhouse. This was a conversation she could have.

"Oh..." Hillary seemed thrown by the comment and started chewing her bottom lip. "We're having everything at the beach, the ceremony and the reception. There will be a tent, in case it rains, and Kathy is making the cake, of course."

Of course. Their aunt Kathy, Sandra and Caroline's mother's youngest sister, ran the best bakery on the Cape. She didn't try to compete with the Sweet Harmony Café; both businesses were considered some of the top spots by tourists and locals alike. Kathy was everyone's favorite aunt, perhaps because she was the youngest, perhaps because she was warm and understanding, or because she knew that sometimes chocolate was the best answer to life's problems.

Right now, Caroline wouldn't mind a long chat with Kathy. She decided to pay her a visit as soon as possible.

"And?" Caroline waited. Surely there must be more, unless Hillary was afraid of rubbing it in and adding salt to Caroline's wounds. "What about a honeymoon?" she asked to prove that she was okay with all of this, hoping that if she tried hard enough, she'd convince herself, too.

The more she asked, the easier it became. It was as if she

was detaching from the role of Caroline, jilted bride, and becoming Caroline, supportive friend and cousin. And... maid of honor.

She felt a wave of dizziness and set a steadying hand on the counter.

"Oh..." Hillary walked over to the assortment of necklaces that Sandra had on display. "You know how Tim is."

Caroline frowned again. Yes, she did know how Tim was, and he wasn't the person she'd once thought him to be. And now she was worried. Was there trouble between Tim and Hillary? Was her cousin having doubts?

"Have you talked to him about it? Have you taken time off from work?" she asked in what she hoped passed for a casual tone.

Hillary's job at the Historical Society could be demanding in the summer months when curious tourists liked to poke in for information about the town's oldest buildings and founders, and surely something like a honeymoon would have to be planned months in advance.

Hillary gave a watery smile in response to that question. "I don't want to nag Tim. I'm sure he has something in mind." But she didn't sound very sure, and the shadow that clouded her eyes made Caroline's stomach knot.

Tim was not a planner; this was true. And she knew from experience that when it came to the wedding, Caroline had to take every detail upon herself or there wouldn't have been a wedding at all.

And still, there hadn't been one, she thought with a silent snort.

Caroline started to speak, but suddenly Hillary lifted her expression into a bright smile.

"Now!" she said, linking Caroline's arm affectionately. "Let's get you into that bridesmaid dress! Oops! I mean, maid of honor!"

It turned out that by getting into the dress, Hillary meant more like stuffing Caroline into it. Despite having a slim figure that she maintained through a rigorous morning workout and long evening walks, the dress clung to her hips, squeezed her stomach, and pushed her cleavage up in a way that made every woman in the room's eyes pop when she stepped in front of the three-way mirror.

"Oh!" There was a flash of alarm on her aunt's face before she quickly composed her expression. Sandra visibly gulped as she hurried toward her with a set of pins. "Oh, I see. I see! Yes, well, let's see what can be done. We'll have to let out the seams…"

Caroline tossed a desperate look at Molly, the more sympathetic one of her two sisters present, but even Molly had to cover her face to hide her laughter.

Caroline, on the other hand, struggled to breathe as her aunt put pins in the dress, marking the places she'd have to alter.

"It might be easier to just start over again," Caroline told her aunt, while the other women went back into their dressing rooms to change into streetwear.

"No time for that!" Sandra's brow pinched with worry

while she continued to inspect the dress. "We have twelve bridesmaids! You four Baker girls, my twins, Kathy's three, and three of Hillary's friends. I'm almost grateful that my brother's two daughters aren't able to come to town for the event. I still have to do the final alterations on all the other dresses and then finish my own mother-of-the-bride gown. And of course, who can forget the bride herself?"

"That sounds like a lot of work," Caroline commented. *And not a lot of time*, she thought to herself.

Sandra was surprisingly quiet as she finished pinning. "I'll get it done. What other choice is there?"

None, Caroline knew, but that didn't mean that it would get done easily, or with joy. And the event planner in her struggled to think of a bride's mother being so stressed leading up to the wedding day. Hillary was the first of Sandra's daughters to be married, and Sandra had talked for years about how much she longed for this day, especially since her own wedding day had been a justice of the peace event—a wedding that had been just as disappointing as the marriage itself.

The days leading up to next Saturday should be filled with anticipation, not worry. Even if that's what Caroline was starting to feel. And not for the reasons others might have thought.

There was something off about this wedding. Something that she was determined to get to the bottom of the next time she got Hillary alone.

The bells above the door jangled, and, startled, Sandra accidentally poked Caroline. She let out a little yelp of pain, but when she saw who was standing in the doorway of the boutique, what she really wanted to do was scream.

Tim—and his brother—stood side by side, looking nothing alike in features, but everything alike in their expression. Both wore a look of shock, and Caroline couldn't even hide her horror until she remembered what she was wearing—and, worse, what was showing.

She'd imagined running into Tim countless times over the years—it was all the more reason not to risk returning to town, even when he was living in Boston and the chances of seeing him were low. In her fantasies, she was brisk, pleasant, and completely unfazed by the presence of the man who had shattered her dreams and her heart in one fell swoop. She barely stopped walking, not willing to give him the time of day, leaving him to stand and watch her go, and wonder if he'd made the biggest mistake of his life.

But she was in no position to walk anywhere right now, and she felt cornered, with the Reynolds brothers blocking her path to the exit and this darn dress making it impossible to even move more than a few inches at a time.

She had no choice but to look at Tim, properly, at the face that she'd tried so hard to forget, even though it was still so achingly familiar. His eyes bore through her, his attention never drifting, and she realized only now that she hadn't felt the heat of his stare in a very long time.

That somewhere along the way, his gaze had started to wander. And she hadn't seen it until now.

"Tim." Her voice felt choked as she tried to splay her fingers over her pounding chest, wondering if the racing of her heart could be heard by anyone else. The shop was quiet enough to hear one of Sandra's pins drop. It was as if no one dared to even breathe.

He was still handsome, with those clear eyes and tousled light brown hair, and when he dared to smile at her, the dimples that he was forever known for—and remembered for—flashed.

Her stomach tightened involuntarily, and she quickly looked around for help.

Sandra, however, had suddenly vanished, but Hillary quickly swept in from the dressing rooms to greet her fiancé.

Her fiancé.

Caroline watched as the man she had grown up with, her first kiss, first love, first everything—even heartbreak—broke into a smile as Hillary moved to take his hand.

It felt so strange, and so wrong, to watch Tim light up at the sight of another woman and then so easily reach out and touch her, when for so long, the only girl he'd ever touched had been Caroline. That's what made them so special, he used to say. They were their firsts and onlys.

So much for that.

It wasn't lost on her that the last time she'd looked into those gray eyes, she'd been madly in love, and now, as she took in that once-irresistible grin and handsome face, she felt nothing but repulsion.

It was better than attraction, she knew. But she wished instead that she felt nothing at all.

Feeling Lucas's scrutiny, Caroline quickly straightened her shoulders, hoping not to look any more bothered by Tim's sudden presence as she was over being dressed like a stuffed turquoise sausage. She hadn't seen Tim since the night before their wedding, a night she had replayed over and over again, looking for a sign she had missed, anything that might have given any indication that Tim had changed his mind, but every time coming up blank. They'd chatted with friends and family at the rehearsal dinner Caroline's parents had thrown them at the house. They'd snuck away for a few stolen moments, both giddy but excited, both seemingly looking forward to the next day, the day that all the ones before it had been leading up to.

He'd kissed her good-night before leaving with Lucas.

She just hadn't known at the time that he was also kissing her goodbye.

Lucas. She narrowed her eyes on the man now, whose dark eyes seemed to have grown a shade deeper. Had he played a part in it? Convinced his brother not to go through with it? Told him he could do better? That he shouldn't marry the first girl he'd ever dated?

Tim looked up to Lucas. Even though they weren't that far apart in age, Lucas had stepped up as the man in the family, been there for his younger brother when their father had moved to Boston, spending more and more time focused on work and less and less time with his sons. Tim would have listened to him.

And Lucas, as evidenced by his actions on the day of her wedding, would do anything for Tim.

"It's nice to see you again, Caroline," Tim said as he and Hillary approached, hand in hand.

What was proper etiquette in this situation? A handshake? Not that Caroline was willing to drop hers from her chest. She'd always thought when this moment came that she'd turn and walk away. Or tell him off, once and for all, because she hadn't the nerve to do it before. Couldn't bear to hear then what she already knew. Couldn't chase him when he was too cowardly to talk to her himself.

But Hillary was looking nervously from Tim to Caroline, her cousins and sisters and aunt were all hiding within eavesdropping distance, and Lucas was staring at her stonily. Caroline saw no choice.

Besides, she had agreed to be a bridesmaid. Maid of honor, actually. To show her support. *Show* being the operative word.

She took in Tim's smug smile, the way he now looped a hand casually around Hillary's waist. He didn't seem to have a care in the world, at least not enough to spare her feelings.

And the last thing Caroline was going to do was give him the satisfaction that any still lingered on her part for him.

"So nice to see you, Tim," she said with her sweetest smile. In her periphery, she saw Lucas's eyes widen. "Hillary was telling me all about your wedding plans. Just a little over a week now! You must be counting the days."

Lucas coughed and then sputtered into his hand. Perhaps it wasn't the right thing to say, all things considered.

"What brings you two here?" Hillary asked, seeming eager to change the topic. Caroline used the opportunity to snatch a scarf from a nearby rack and throw it over her shoulders. Who cared if it was plaid and made of wool?

She felt Lucas's eyes on her as she covered herself, but she focused on Hillary, the entire reason that she was suffering through this humiliation. Hillary, whose favorite necklace for years was the half heart whose match was around Caroline's neck, who always offered to trade half her sandwich because Sandra gave her ham and American cheese and Caroline's mother gave her heirloom tomato with arugula and goat cheese—something she didn't appreciate until she was well into high school.

Even back then, they were sharing everything. Caroline had just never thought one day they'd share the same man.

Same fiancé.

"You mentioned you'd be here, so I thought I'd try my luck," Tim said, snuggling Hillary closer.

Caroline was all too aware that her eyes bulged before she could stop herself—by the sheer awkwardness and the audacity. Was he deliberately trying to get a rise out of her?

Or had he simply moved on and assumed she had, too?

Caroline accidentally glanced at Lucas, whose dark stare never seemed to waver.

"I wanted to see if you're free for drinks tonight," Tim went on. "Bring your sisters and cousins, too. The more the merrier."

He had the nerve to look at Caroline. Was he inviting her to hang out, as if the last time they'd seen each other *they* hadn't been the ones about to be married? Did he not remember that once, they, too, had an exciting week leading up to their wedding, complete with drinks and showers, toasts, and celebrations, everyone laughing, everyone congratulating the happy couple?

Next to him, Lucas looked pale, his eyes darker than ever.

Caroline was about to tell Tim exactly where to stuff that invitation, but Hillary said, "We'd love to! Wouldn't we,

Caroline? And all the girls, of course!" She stared at Caroline hopefully.

"Oh, I—" But then Caroline caught Tim's gaze and saw the hint of a smile pass over his lips, and what else could she do but agree or look like she still had a problem with the man her cousin was marrying? It had been three years. People *had* moved on.

Even if all she'd done was move away.

"I'd love to. Now, if you'll excuse me," Caroline managed. "I need to change out of this dress."

She started to walk toward the dressing room, forgetting that she'd had to all but hop from it when she'd emerged, and in her haste, she took a huge stride, and the sound of fabric ripping filled the small store.

She closed her eyes as her cheeks grew hot, but then she lifted her chin and, with as much dignity as she could muster, took what felt like two hundred baby steps to the dressing room door, where sure enough, Sandra, Valerie, Molly, Phoebe, and Kyla were huddled together, hiding from the drama.

They may as well have made a bowl of popcorn while they were at it.

Caroline gave them each a scolding look, but then she just sighed.

After all, who could blame them? If she'd had the option of hiding out, she would have.

But instead, she was back here. Trying to be here for her family.

She just hadn't realized that her effort extended to

Hillary, who she suspected might need her even more than her parents did.

Lucas fumed the entire walk to the Bayview Inn, where he was meeting Wallace. He'd accompanied his brother to the dress shop because he had a bad feeling that Tim would run into Caroline there—and he needed to do damage control if he did. He hadn't told his brother that he'd seen Caroline, or that she was a bridesmaid, either. He figured that Hillary would be the one to share those details. So when Tim announced he wanted to stop by and surprise Hillary before taking her to lunch, a hundred thoughts went through Lucas's mind, and none of them were good. He didn't know what his brother was playing at, inviting Caroline out for drinks! Had he assumed she'd say no, or was he actually hoping that she'd say yes?

And she had done just that. Called his bluff, perhaps.

Or maybe... Lucas clenched his jaw. He couldn't even entertain the thought of Caroline still having feelings for Tim.

Not when he had other problems to deal with right now.

His heart pounded with each step toward the historic mansion owned by Hillary and Caroline's aunt, Kathy Hayward, the agreed-upon place for his lunch meeting. The only comfort he took was knowing that the worst, he supposed, was over with now that Tim and his ex had come face-to-face. Nothing had been thrown, names hadn't been called, and tears hadn't been shed.

It had all been perfectly civil.

He supposed he should have warned Tim that Caroline was back in town. The shock on his brother's face confirmed that Tim hadn't been tipped off about Caroline's return—and the show of affection he made to his current fiancée did nothing to ease Lucas's worries about any lingering feelings toward the former one.

Tim might not have been able to go through with marrying Caroline, but Lucas didn't believe that had anything to do with his lack of emotions for her.

And that was just the problem. One of many.

And right now, as he walked up the short steps and opened the door to the Bayview Inn, he had to focus on the one at hand.

"Lucas!" Wallace Hadley was standing near the original hearth that anchored the lobby of the historic inn. A large man with a booming voice and balding head, he pulled the attention of a few guests who were reading in armchairs, and a couple who was passing through on their way to the bistro. The expensive suit might have had something to do with it; Harmony Cove was a laidback town, one that appealed to tourists and small business owners. Business meetings here usually involved a coffee at Sweet Harmony or a round of golf at the nearby course.

But here Lucas was, in his best summer suit. Anxiously, he adjusted his tie as he crossed the worn floorboards to greet the man who held his entire fate in his hands.

Lucas extended a hand and the older man gave it a robust shake. It was only their third time meeting—unlike the other investors whom Tim had brought on the ninth hole, Lucas alone had garnered Wallace's support of the project, but it hadn't come easily, and despite having a signed contract, it still didn't feel permanent.

There were too many loopholes in Wallace's favor, too many ways his lawyers would be able to get him—and his money—out of the project.

And that would grind the entire hotel to a halt.

And be the end of Reynolds Properties.

The two men moved into the back of the inn, where the cozy restaurant was bustling with locals and tourists. The French doors were open, letting the breeze blow in off the bay, and they were quickly escorted by Kathy's husband, Joe, to a table on the patio with a coveted view of Harmony Harbor.

This lunch, however, would be far from relaxing. And Lucas knew that Wallace wasn't here to enjoy the scenery.

They placed orders for iced teas and lobster rolls and made some brief small talk about Wallace's upcoming vacation plans to the Outer Banks before getting to the purpose of the visit.

"You know, of course, that we broke ground," Lucas said proudly, referencing the email he'd sent out to inform all of his investors on the status of the project. "I'm happy to give you a tour of the building site after lunch if you don't need to get back to Boston too soon."

"I've already toured the site," Wallace surprised him by saying. "I stopped over there on my way here. I was surprised to find neither you nor your brother anywhere to be seen."

Lucas resisted the urge to loosen his tie. He felt out of place dressed so formally on such a warm day in what was considered by most to be a resort town, the very reason why he chose to build his signature property here, among more personal motives.

He'd been at work since seven, long before the crew had shown up, but Wallace had likely passed by when Lucas chose to accompany his brother to the dress shop to do damage control.

Trying to manage one problem led only to a new one.

"I must have stepped out for a meeting," he said simply. "I can assure you that I'm married to the job."

Wallace's smile was thin. "Marriage is a wonderful institution. Maureen and I just celebrated our fortieth anniversary."

"Congratulations," Lucas said, meaning it. It was no small feat, certainly more than his parents had managed, and more than he'd ever hope for—or try for.

Wallace eyed him. "We were at a fundraising event this past weekend. We saw your father."

"Ah." The real reason for this meeting, then. Bruce Reynolds ran in the same circles as the likes of Wallace Hadley; it was the warm lead that had granted Lucas the original meeting with the wealthy investor. It was also the reason for endless restrictions in the contract.

Reynolds Properties may not be owned and operated by Lucas's father anymore, but his reputation still tarnished it.

"He was with a woman who, funny enough, used to play dolls with one of my granddaughters." Wallace's expression said that there was, however, nothing amusing about this at all. "And his hand was on her rear end."

Lucas managed not to sigh. The older and wealthier his

father became, the younger the women he seemed to date. After his second divorce, he never had another serious relationship, instead choosing to keep casual company, to the point where Lucas could no longer keep up with their names.

"I haven't seen my father in a while," Lucas said in response. Since moving back to Harmony Cove from Boston full-time over the winter, he'd barely spoken to the man, either. His father had never been one for traditional holidays, and once he'd retired from the business, they didn't seem to have much more reason to communicate.

Judging from Wallace's expression, it wasn't the correct answer.

"I'm not here to judge anyone," Wallace said. "But I also won't put myself in a position to be judged by my association with people who don't uphold my personal values. My wife is up for president of the board of a very prominent charitable organization, and this comes with scrutiny."

"I understand," Lucas said, the acid in his stomach burning.

"As you know, I had my doubts about investing in Reynolds Properties," Wallace went on, stopping only to let the server deliver their food. He took a big bite of his sandwich and chewed while eyeing Lucas. "I don't like funny business, and I don't like risks. Discretion in business is as important as it is in personal matters. I like to put my money into something I believe in, and that's not just about the bottom line. I think you know what I mean, Lucas."

Lucas did. The Hadleys were reputable people. They had

a name to uphold. One they didn't want to be dragged down by behavior that they didn't agree with—or respect.

"My father retired from the business over a year ago," Lucas reminded Wallace. "As I promised you in our first meeting, Reynolds Properties is entering a new generation. My brother and I have taken over, and we're excited about the new direction."

Even if it was a struggle. They'd inherited a dying business. Lucas often thought that was the only reason that their father was willing to walk away from it. They'd been draining money for years since people started vacating office properties and seldom returned. There was no need for more developments, and the properties that they continued to manage were half-empty at best.

Banks wouldn't loan to them anymore. Enter the need for the likes of Wallace Hadley.

"I'm not talking about a shift from office buildings to hotels, Lucas," Wallace grumbled. He took another large bite of his food, grunting with approval, clearly enjoying that much of his visit, at least.

Lucas couldn't bring himself to touch his plate. Wallace hadn't come out to the Cape for a friendly chat. If he'd taken time out of his week to make the trek and face the traffic, then he was bothered enough to consider pulling out of the project.

Just when they'd broken ground.

Meaning bills would have to be paid. And there wouldn't be enough money in the bank to cover the costs.

"We're not the same company," Lucas said firmly. "My father had his vices. Believe me, I witnessed them firsthand."

His jaw clenched when he thought of his father's ways, both professionally and personally. The assistants he'd briefly dated or slept with, some while married to his mother. The stories Lucas heard once he started working for the company after college. His father had no problems cheating on his wife, cheating at cards, and cheating in business when it came to putting an extra penny in his bank account. He'd cut corners where it benefited him, and he was known to play dirty when it came to getting past building regulations, too.

"And I learned a lot from him." He looked Wallace square in the eye. "I play by the book, Wallace, just like I told you in our first meeting. You won't have to worry about any rumors if you hitch your wagon to the Reynolds name, sir. I'm a man of my word. And I promise you that you can count on us to uphold the values that will be associated with this resort."

Wallace stared at him for a long moment as if considering whether or not to believe him. "It's a family resort, at least that's how you sold it to me. It's the only reason I agreed to put my money into the project. But people won't buy into it if management is run by a bunch of philanderers, Lucas."

Lucas swallowed back his iced tea. Hard.

"We're a new generation," Lucas assured him. "With different values."

Wallace's gaze was steady for an unnerving amount of time. "You just said that you haven't seen your father in a long time. How does that align with this wholesome family resort you're pitching to the public? People will see through to corporate greed if you're not buying what you're selling."

"We're a family company and we always will be. And we

have a family event next week, in fact," Lucas said lightly, even as his collar began to itch. "My younger brother, Tim, is getting married right here in our hometown."

Wallace's bushy eyebrows shot up in pleased surprise. "Why didn't you mention this?"

Lucas's smile felt forced. "I guess I've been too busy getting the hotel going."

Wallace leaned forward. "Son, there is nothing more important than family, you hear me?"

For lack of any other appropriate response, Lucas nodded.

"So, a wedding! Next Saturday?" Wallace happily went back to his food. "Maureen and I will be there. We never miss a wedding."

Lucas was suddenly aware he was gaping and quickly clamped his mouth closed. His heart was slamming against his ribs and his breath felt strangled, and he knew that under any other circumstances, it would be perfectly reasonable for Wallace and his wife to attend his brother's wedding.

But this was Tim they were talking about. Tim Reynolds.

And like Wallace was so keen to point out and concerned enough to voice, the Reynoldses were not known for their upstanding reputation.

They were not known for being men that women could rely on.

Or that people like Wallace Hadley could, either.

But Lucas would be damned if he let his father or his brother ruin this opportunity for him. It wasn't just the first big project since he'd taken over the company. It was his vision. Here, in Harmony Cove.

It was the project that had taken him home and could keep him here, doing what he loved, in the place he loved. Doing it all so much differently than the man before him.

"I give you my word," he said firmly, "that I will do everything it takes to ensure that the Grand Harmony Hotel is a success."

Even if that meant he had to drag his brother to the altar and say the words *I do* for him.

Four

Instead of stopping into Sweet Harmony for a much-needed chat with her mother, Caroline took a long walk along the bayfront to calm her nerves and recover from seeing Tim, but even the lull of the waves crashing against the shoreline didn't work their magic today. She was still shaken by the time she wandered around the back of her aunt's inn, past a hedge of hydrangeas just starting to bloom.

Her father was waiting for her when she arrived at the side door to the Bayview Bistro, and much to her relief, he looked exactly the same as he had when she'd seen him last summer. No new haircut for him. He was still her dad in every sense of the word, from his sensible khaki pants to his leather boat shoes, to the golf shirt he liked to wear in the warmer weather, replacing the plaid ones he wore in the cooler months.

He greeted her with a big smile that met his blue eyes and a long, warm hug that seemed to melt away all of her heartache and worries, at least for the moment.

There was no place better than in her father's arms. It was more her home than this town or that ramshackle old house where he no longer resided.

"Aren't you a sight." Mitch's voice was hoarse when he pulled back.

Any worry Caroline had felt for her father disappeared when she saw how well he looked. There was color in his cheeks, and he hadn't traded in his wire glasses for colored contacts. No signs of a midlife crisis, unlike her mother. His eyes gleamed, and his smile seemed genuine, not strained.

"You look good, Dad," she said honestly, and more than a little surprised.

"I am good," he said, grinning wider.

Was he really? Caroline hated to think of him being miserable, but could he really be this happy separated from his wife of thirty-five years? The one he used to dance with in the kitchen and pick flowers for at random?

"So retirement suits you?" she asked carefully. Once, there had been a time when none of them could have imagined a day when Mitch Baker wasn't sitting behind his big wooden desk at the family newspaper he'd inherited from his father, but then there had also been a time when no one would have imagined Mitch living in the attic of the *Harmony Herald*, either.

"I've kept busy," he said. "I've been making some new plans. Ones I'm not quite ready to share yet. I'm still...fine-tuning a few things."

"I missed you, Dad," Caroline said, hugging him again, feeling the tears threaten to spill when she pulled back and looked into his moist eyes.

"Me too, Princess." He pulled in a shaky breath and then rallied, bending his elbow to take her arm and leading her into the side entrance directly into the restaurant. "Now, tell me all about your news!"

"Spoken like a true journalist," she said with a laugh.

"I may have retired but I haven't changed," her father replied.

And thank God for that, Caroline thought.

She was still smiling when they pushed through the door—and straight into the chest of none other than Lucas Reynolds.

The smile immediately fell from her face as she stared into his stony expression. One quick glance assured her that he was alone, or at least only with an older gentleman who she didn't recognize. Another person might have joked, *Twice in one day!* Even in Harmony Cove, it was uncommon. But Lucas wasn't the teasing kind. And Caroline was in no laughing mood.

With a racing heart, she looked over her shoulder for any sign of Tim, but Lucas simply nodded in acknowledgment and then stepped aside to let her and her father pass, whom he greeted with a quick handshake.

The disdain must have still shown on Caroline's face after the door had closed because her father gave her a wink of camaraderie.

"Mitch! And…Caroline?"

Caroline looked over to see her aunt Kathy hurrying across the crowded dining room toward them, her arms outstretched until she finally pulled Caroline close to her and kept her there for a moment. Any lingering anxiety over having seen Tim dissipated. Aunt Kathy was a favorite of all the cousins, and rightfully so. She was funny and kind, maternal and sisterly at the same time. She was, as Val liked to say when they were younger, a "cooler" version of their mother.

She was also fiercely protective of those she loved.

"I heard you were back! Oh, let me look at you! Still pretty as a picture!" Her dark eyes roamed over Caroline's face before she went back for another squeeze.

All thoughts of Lucas were momentarily discarded by her aunt's greeting until Kathy pulled back and narrowed her gaze. "I hope that Reynolds boy wasn't bothering you."

He was hardly a boy anymore, Caroline thought, unable to stop herself from picturing the image of a man filling out a nicely cut suit.

"He was just leaving when we came in," Caroline assured her aunt, grateful for the support. "Besides, I can't let him or his brother bother me, can I? They're going to be family now."

Kathy's eyes widened dramatically in a way that said she had much to say on that subject but that now was probably not that time.

"We *must* catch up," she whispered.

Caroline nodded. "We will. I'll stop by the bakery soon."

Kathy and her husband owned the inn as their primary business, with the on-site bakery being Kathy's side project and the restaurant being Joe's. On busy summer afternoons like this one, it was all hands on deck, though, and Caroline was sure that her cousin Lucy was scrambling to keep up with the demand in the bakery at the other end of the property.

Kathy led them to their table, and Caroline thought she was doing a good job of relaxing when they reached the patio, where the water glistened in the near distance, and the sun shone warmly on her face, but she could sense that her dad was worried when he looked at her.

She quickly smiled, determined to show that all was right in her world, even when it was so far from it. She was back in town to see what was going on in her parents' lives, to understand this marital separation, and to see if she, being the oldest and, in her opinion, the most level-headed of the Baker sisters, could perhaps help mediate a resolution.

She may not have found love and she may not believe that it lasted for most, but if any two people belonged together, it was her parents.

Surely there was an explanation. Like her mother's pink highlights!

"Lunch on the patio of the Bayview Bistro with one of the prettiest girls in town." Her father had a twinkle in his eye. "It doesn't get much better than this. And it certainly beats a sandwich back at my desk—or table, seeing as I don't exactly have an office anymore."

Caroline wanted to point out that lunch with his wife would surely top anything, but instead she said, "This is a long overdue celebration for your retirement. My treat, of course."

"No!" Mitch immediately frowned.

"Please, Dad, I insist." Then, teasing, she said, "Or I won't eat a thing."

"Business going that well?" he remarked.

Caroline's pause was brief. She was here to worry about him, not the other way around.

"Very!" she said brightly. "So, please. My treat."

"You always were stubborn," he replied with an easy smile. "I won't say no, but I will say thank you. It isn't every day that I have the honor of lunching with my oldest daughter. Isn't this nice, just the two of us?"

Caroline hesitated. It was nice. On one hand, she craved this, one-on-one attention, when so often growing up she'd have to share her father with one of her sisters or, of course, her mother. It was a rare occasion when it was just the two of them, not counting those first two and a half years of her life before Annie came along, a time when she was too young to remember.

But she would enjoy having her father all to herself much more if she knew that later they'd be sitting down to a big family dinner, like old times. On summer days like this, they'd gather at the picnic table on the lawn, with a platter of buttery corn on the cob, a salad made from the vegetables in her mother's garden, and herbed bread baked fresh and still warm from the oven.

Better than all the food, though, was the company. There would be conversation, everyone talking over each other, and everyone laughing as the sun went down and the stars came out. By the end of the night, there would be full bellies.

And full hearts.

And right now, Caroline felt like hers was breaking.

"I suppose that since you're back, you've heard..." Her father hesitated, giving her a nervous glance.

Her smile was reassuring, even if it did little to make her feel better about the situation. "I've heard, yes, and as it turns out, I'm not just attending the wedding but I'm going to be in it."

Her father's eyebrows arched.

"Are you sure that's a good idea?" His forehead crinkled with concern.

Caroline wasn't sure of anything. Not the wedding. Not her part in it. Not Hillary's decision to go through with it.

Not Tim's ability to do the same.

She wasn't sure about her business, or how to keep it going, especially now that Maya had left her for a steady, secure job.

And she wasn't even sure that she had her family to fall back on, like she always did, because they had fractured in her time away, and she didn't know if there was anything she could do or say to put them back together again.

"I'm not here to discuss me, Dad. I'm worried about you," she said.

"Oh, honey, you have no reason to be. I'm doing just fine. Great, really," he assured her, and Caroline was both surprised and a little disturbed to find that he sounded like he meant it.

"Great? But—"

But he was living above the newspaper offices instead in their beautiful, albeit cluttered home. He was probably eating cereal for dinner instead of salads with produce fresh from Sharon's garden, or the homecooked berry pies that she always made for desserts this time of year. They'd met here at the Bistro instead of the café for a reason. And while Caroline was perfectly happy to support her aunt and uncle's business, she knew that Sweet Harmony was their second home. Or that it had been once.

"I know about you and Mom," she said gently.

Her father sighed heavily and then gave a small smile. "No matter what happens with your mother and me, it doesn't change how we feel about you girls. We're always right here for you, and I hope you know that."

A lump formed in her throat. "I know, Dad. But..."

But she just wanted everything to go back to the way it was.

And she was experienced enough to know that wishes didn't always come true and that love didn't always last.

"It all feels...different," she said sadly.

Her father reached across the table and took one of her hands, squeezing it in his.

"Sometimes you just have to have trust that everything will be okay," he said.

Caroline stared at her father for a long time, wanting to tell him that she could do that, but not wanting to promise something she couldn't.

She'd lost her trust a very long time ago, when someone she'd loved had broken it.

Annie had never made it to the dress shop, but Caroline knew that she'd find her at the office of the family newspaper, where her father was headed anyway. Even though he had officially retired, as expected, he couldn't resist writing the occasional freelance piece, and Caroline suspected that he missed the company. The *Harmony Herald* had been in the Baker family for four generations. Caroline felt her heart swell when she stopped outside the front door and saw that the plaque had been changed to list her sister as the editor-in-chief.

Make that co-editor-in-chief. Caroline paused to look at Sean Morrison's name, still surprised to think that he'd found his way back to Harmony Cove.

And into her sister's life.

She could remember her sister's heartache as fresh as her own. When Sean broke up with her to move to DC, choosing his career over their relationship, prioritizing success over this town, his own life over a future together, Annie had sworn off love and eventually this town, too. But now he was back, not just at the paper where he'd gotten his first byline, but in Annie's life, it would seem.

Caroline didn't know how she felt about that.

Concerned, she supposed. Confused. More than a little cynical, if she was being honest. Why would Annie think that this time things would be any different? Sean had been willing to give up on her and the paper once before—what made her think that he'd changed his ways?

What made her think that this time she could trust him to stay?

Aunt Marcy shuffled down the hallway after Caroline left her father in search of Annie. In the three years since Caroline had last been in town, Marcy hadn't changed, and that was quite literally. In her hand was her beloved cat mug, whose handle was in the shape of a feline tail, despite Marcy having never owned a pet due to allergies, and Caroline recognized the hand-knitted pink cardigan with the jewel buttons that she seemed to wear daily around the office to ward off the chill (from the draft in the winter and from the window air-conditioning units in the summer) when it wasn't otherwise draped over the back of her chair. If it was ever washed, Caroline didn't know and was honestly afraid to ask.

"Why, Caroline!" Marcy's wide blue eyes grew even rounder behind her thick glasses, which seemed to magnify her permanently curious expression. "I heard you were back in town!"

Of course. Marcy made it her business to hear everything, whether she was intended to or not.

Caroline couldn't help but smile at the sight of her father's younger and only sister. She leaned forward and hugged the plump woman, breathing in the scent of the perfume she'd worn for as long as Caroline could remember.

"I must say, I was surprised to learn that you'd be attending Hillary's wedding," Marcy remarked when they pulled away. She stared at Caroline in that particular way of hers, not blinking, head tilted patiently and sympathetically, aching for more information.

Marcy was easy to open up to, which was why most people eventually did. She was a shoulder to cry on at the local watering hole after one too many glasses of chardonnay and a messy argument with a spouse, the perfect listener in the produce aisle at the market, after a tense schoolboard meeting where no one could agree if a certain principal who would not be named should be retained after hiring his recent girlfriend over the much more qualified, and admittedly less attractive and married with six children, Mrs. Shoudy, and the supportive friend to anyone over at the café who needed to bend an ear about anything from husbands who drank too much, wives who spent too much, husbands who lost jobs, managers who were about to let people go from their positions, and everything in between.

Most of it ended up in Marcy's Harmony Happenings column, a community favorite, not that any well-respected local would ever admit it. Caroline's father would flick past his sister's column with a burdened sigh, while the sisters stifled giggles and then smuggled the morning edition up to their room to read it with pleasure, over and over again, trying to decipher their aunt's code: if a "certain unnamed man with wire glasses" might be Mr. Murphy, who ran the hardware store, or Mr. Charles down at the lobster shack. They ruled their own father out; his were reading glasses, and he'd never stack up gambling debts playing late-night poker!

As Caroline grew older, she grew more wary of her aunt's column, and when she got stood up on her wedding day, well, she grew downright scared.

And rightfully so.

"Hillary and I have always been as close as sisters," she said to her aunt in response to her fishing.

"Still..." Marcy waggled her eyebrows suggestively. Then, as she was prone to do, she pulled a deeply sympathetic face and set a hand on Caroline's wrist. "I just know how hard this must be for you. What with everything that happened."

Caroline wanted to believe that her aunt was just being

caring. Marcy wasn't cruel, after all. But she was a reporter. And a gossip columnist at that.

And Caroline refused to give anyone in this town the satisfaction of thinking that she was still affected by what happened to her three years ago—especially Tim Reynolds himself.

"That was years ago, Aunt Marcy. I'm fine now, really. Better than fine, actually." She smiled brightly, hoping that she wasn't selling it too hard when she saw the suspicious narrowing of her aunt's eyes. Toning it down a little, she said, "I have a great business. With a great friend." No need to add the truth here. Her aunt didn't need to know what was really going on in Philadelphia, only here in Harmony Cove.

"That's great, dear," Marcy eventually said, giving her an encouraging smile. "And did I hear that you're going to be the maid of honor?"

Boy, Marcy sure didn't miss a thing! That had been confirmed only a matter of hours ago!

Caroline nodded. "That's right. If Sandra can get the dress finished in time."

"Oh, I'm sure she'll make it happen. It's not her that I'm worried about..."

Caroline frowned at her aunt. "What's that supposed to mean?"

Marcy bristled and then fluttered her hand in front of her face as if fanning herself. "Forget I said anything. I'm just getting overwhelmed thinking of all the details that must go into a wedding with such short notice that's all. If I didn't know better, I'd think there was a reason for such a rush, if you know what I mean." She waggled her eyebrows, and Caroline's stomach lurched. "But I do know better. Because I make it my concern to know everything that happens in town. I'm very close friends with the receptionist at the local doctor's office..." she added in a whisper.

Meaning that Hillary was not having a so-called "shotgun" wedding. Still, Marcy had raised a good point. If there was no pregnancy, why the urgency? From what Caroline knew, and she had tried to learn as little as possible admittedly, Hillary and Tim hadn't been dating long—far less than a year. The engagement had been quick, but the wedding was even quicker.

And Caroline couldn't help but wonder what Tim was thinking—and if she had a reason to be worried for her cousin.

"Word on the street is that you and Tim saw each other today," Marcy remarked, widening her eyes a notch. She held them like that, not blinking.

Caroline stifled a sigh, feeling no option but to give in to her aunt's curiosity.

"It was perfectly civil," she said truthfully. "I'm sorry I can't tell you something juicier."

Marcy pulled a look of disappointment. "Darn. I was rather hoping that he finally got what he deserved."

Caroline glanced wistfully out the window at the end of the hall, the one with the view of the town, entertaining that very thought, though given Marcy's flair for exaggeration, she couldn't be sure that their visions quite matched.

"It would seem that Tim has found his happy ending," she said decisively.

While she... She had given up searching for hers.

"Has he?" Marcy raised a single eyebrow, causing Caroline to frown. "Anyway, I'm off. I'm chasing a story before my deadline."

Caroline could only imagine which poor soul was the subject of this column. So long as it wasn't her, she supposed that she could breathe easily.

"It was nice seeing you, Aunt Marcy," she said, meaning it.

"You, too, dear. And I'll see you soon. You're in town through the wedding, at least. Please don't be a stranger!"

Caroline shook her head. "I won't," she promised. And she meant it. She'd finally found the courage to come back to Harmony Cove. She'd faced Tim. What more was there to hide from after this?

And what was waiting for her back in Philly?

With a pit in her stomach, she waved goodbye to her aunt and knocked on Annie's old office door, the one she'd occupied before heartache had driven her out of town, too.

But now she was back, settled not just in her hometown but at her old desk, where she belonged, and Caroline couldn't help but feel an ache in her chest when she wondered where she belonged.

Because it certainly wasn't Philadelphia. But was it here? Could she ever really build a life for herself here when the one she'd planned was taken from her so abruptly?

"Come in!" Annie's voice was muffled behind the closed door.

"Look at you!" Caroline quickened her steps to hug her sister. They talked on the phone sporadically, both busy with their careers, but this was the first time they'd been face-to-face since Annie had moved to Seattle. Her sister's long auburn hair was pulled back in a low bun, giving her a look of confidence and seniority, but it was her blue eyes shining with joy that took Caroline aback for a moment. Her sister was happy. Again. And as happy as she was for her, Caroline longed to feel so content herself.

"You look amazing!" she commented. "Seattle clearly had a good effect on you."

"More like moving back did," Annie corrected her. "I missed this place."

Caroline fell silent. She hadn't dared to admit it to herself, but she missed the Cape, too, especially in the summertime when she longed to walk barefoot along the beach, the salty breeze in her hair. She felt trapped at times in Philly, wishing to be out on a boat at sunset, letting her legs dangle over the side, the coastline visible in the distance, reassured in knowing that everyone she loved was within sight.

Of her sisters, Caroline was closest to Annie, maybe because of their proximity in age, or maybe because of what they'd both been through personally. She knew that she could confide in her about what was going on with her business and her once again uncertain future.

But now Marcy was back, claiming she had forgotten her notebook, when in fact all she was doing was standing there watching them, silently observing, no doubt she even had a recording device tucked into her pocket, and so Caroline decided to save a more personal conversation for another day.

Their father popped his head around the open door.

"Why don't I do a coffee run for us?" he suggested.

"Can you grab some of those lemon cookies Mom makes too?" Caroline asked, thinking of the café's beloved seasonal treat, but then stopped when she saw the shadow that fell over her father's face.

"I usually go to Common Grounds," he said, recovering his smile, which did seem strained this time. "But they make a great brownie."

Remembering how it felt to cram herself into that bridesmaid dress, Caroline shook her head. "I'd better not. I have a dress to squeeze into, and I'll have to lose five pounds by next week if I plan to walk down the aisle."

"You sound just like a bride!" Marcy giggled, sneaking up behind her brother, and Annie shook her head, darting a warning look at their aunt, who quickly scurried away—but likely not out of earshot. It was Caroline's father who looked worried.

"Are you okay with everything, sweetie?" he asked, and the look in his eyes was one of such love, such concern, that Caroline wanted nothing more than to take that worry away.

"Sure," she said with a firm nod. "It's been years, Dad. I've built a life for myself."

Or she'd tried. She gave her father a reassuring pat on the arm before he slipped away, in search of coffee from a shop that couldn't top Sweet Harmony because he no longer felt welcome there.

"Did you talk to Mom yet?" Annie asked in a low tone.

"Not yet," Caroline said. "She had book club last night—"

"Book club?" Marcy was suddenly back, looking stricken. "Book club was last week! I should know."

Of course she should. She knew everything.

Caroline frowned at her sister, who didn't argue their aunt's point. "Maybe I misheard…"

Only now she understood perfectly well. Her mother hadn't been honest with her.

Maybe she was simply avoiding Caroline and the inevitable conversation. It was a Baker family trait to hide from problems and difficult conversations, after all.

Annie nudged her chin toward her office, and Caroline said another quick goodbye to Marcy before slipping inside and closing the door.

"So," Annie whispered because they both knew that a closed door couldn't stop Marcy. She'd been known to fetch a glass—more than once. "How are you, really? Marcy filled me in on what happened at the dress shop this morning."

"Just *how* did she find out?" Caroline asked, dropping into a visitor's chair.

Annie could only shrug. "I'm technically her boss and even I don't understand how she does it." They shared a smile. "But seriously, how are you handling all of this?"

Caroline pulled in a big breath, feeling like she could finally shed her armor for a moment. "Oh, other than recovering from the shock of just seeing Tim while I was wearing a dress tighter than sausage casing, I'd say that I'm better than ever."

"No." Annie smothered a laugh with her hand. "I'm sorry."

"No apology needed." Caroline wished she could find

humor in this, and someday she might, but today she was too tired. And the day wasn't even over. She still had to put on a game face for drinks tonight, where she planned to make a quick appearance and nothing more. "Tim and Lucas stopped by the boutique while we were having our fitting."

"And how was that?" Annie looked as mesmerized as Marcy would, had she been allowed in the room.

Caroline glanced at the door, noticing a shadow pass underneath. Clearly, Marcy had decided that family drama would be more titillating than whatever gossip she was chasing.

Lowering her voice further, she leaned across the desk. "I didn't really have much time to process it. I was honestly too distracted by hoping that I wouldn't pop out of the top of the dress."

"The bridesmaid you're replacing was extremely petite," Annie said with a shake of her head when she finished laughing. "But seeing Tim, after all this time. Did you guys speak? Did he..."

"Apologize?" Caroline had long since given up holding out for that. Besides, what did it matter now? She shook her head. "We barely spoke. They just stopped in to invite everyone to drinks tonight."

"Hillary called and mentioned it," Annie said. "But I can make an excuse for you if you want."

Caroline appreciated that but said, "No, it's okay. I'll go. It's the only way to show Tim that he can't hurt me anymore. That I'm over him. And...it's the only way to show Hillary that I'm happy for her. And I want to be, but..."

"But she's marrying the man who left you at the altar without an explanation?"

"Pretty much." Caroline managed a smile.

"You don't have to be her maid of honor, Caroline," Annie said. "She had a lot of nerve asking, if you ask me."

Caroline thought about it for a moment and then shrugged. "Maybe, but this is her wedding, even if it is to Tim. And growing up, we always told each other we'd be part of each other's weddings. Maybe she wanted to uphold the promise, even under the circumstances."

"You two were always close." Annie didn't sound jealous, because she had no reason to be. She understood the bond Hillary and Caroline had, one that was different from sisterhood, but one that was sometimes just as complicated.

Eager to get off the topic that only made her stomach tighten with nerves, Caroline looked around the office, which hadn't changed much since Annie used to work here. "I didn't see Sean when I came in."

"He's meeting with the mayor about the new hotel project. It's been a real newsworthy topic recently."

"Ah, yes, the entire reason the Reynolds brothers are back in town." Caroline couldn't hide her displeasure, but Annie's expression was dreamy. Caroline gaped at her sister as she leaned forward in her chair. "You've really fallen for Sean again!"

She couldn't make sense of this. Forgiving Sean Morrison was one thing, moving on, sure. But Annie and Sean had been high school and college sweethearts. They'd been inseparable for years, both sharing the same passions. The same goals.

Until Sean had gone and thrown it all away. He'd chosen a career over Annie. Over the future they'd planned. He'd cut her out of the vision.

Didn't she remember that? The tears she'd shed? The heartbreak? The anger?

"Maybe I never fell out of love with him," Annie said simply.

"Even after what he did to you?" Caroline knew that it was all too possible to love someone you shouldn't. She'd been more than guilty of that herself.

Annie hesitated for a moment and then said, "I think if love is true, then two people can find a way back to each other."

Caroline thought about this for a moment, knowing better than to impose her own cynicism onto her well-meaning sister and daring to hope that in this instance, Annie was right. Not for her own sake.

But for her parents'.

Lucas nursed his first beer while another round was delivered to the table. Beer for the guys, white wine for the women. He glanced around the patio as he took another sip, telling himself that it was absolutely for the best that Caroline was a no-show tonight. The last thing he needed was for her to sit down and make trouble—or worse, to make Tim start rethinking his decision, past and present.

Valerie was here, and a bunch of Hillary's other cousins, too, and Sean had texted to say that he was putting tomorrow's edition to bed and would be by shortly. It was just as well, Lucas decided. He'd finish this drink and make an excuse to leave early. Hopefully taking Tim with him. With a little over a week to go before the wedding, and now with Wallace Hadley planning to be in attendance, the tighter rein he kept on his brother the better.

He glanced at the door again, but this time he sat up a little straighter when he saw Sean walk in with Annie—and Caroline.

He darted his gaze to his brother, gauging his reaction as he had at the dress shop earlier that day, hoping that he didn't see anything in Tim's expression that revealed regret. He was with Hillary now. He'd made his choice. Then and now. And it was about time that Tim learned to stick with his choices. For better or for worse.

The table was crowded, and after stopping to greet everyone, Lucas stood to help Sean drag three extra chairs to the table. He'd purposefully sat at the opposite end of the table from Tim, wanting to observe from afar where it would be easier to get away with one drink and calling it an early night. Now, he sat back down again only to realize that Caroline was right beside him.

"Oh." His throat tightened, and he took a sip of his beer, one that made up for barely drinking anything for the last hour. She unnerved him, and not only because it was clear that she hadn't forgiven him for his part in her wedding. Caroline was smart and funny and, with her silky blond hair and sparkling blue eyes, more than a little pretty. How a guy like his brother had managed to snag a girl like her had always mystified him, but then, that was Tim's way. He could charm anyone, including the hotel investors, which Lucas was thankful for. But it was the follow-through where he lapsed. Every single time.

Lucas looked over at his brother now, then to Hillary. Not this time. Not if he could help it.

"Wine?" Lucas asked Caroline and Annie after Sean helped himself to one of the beers on the table. He reached for the bottle and poured them each a glass.

"Thank you," Caroline said tightly, not even meeting his gaze. He couldn't blame her. Not after what he'd done.

"I've been hoping to talk to you," he said, lowering his voice so that they wouldn't be heard. "I never had a chance to tell you—"

Caroline turned to him sharply, and he couldn't stop himself from noticing how the soft evening light brought out the pinkness of her cheeks and lips.

"What happened was a long time ago," she said tightly. "Besides, this is Hillary's wedding week, and I'm here to support her. I suppose you've heard by now that I've been promoted to maid of honor."

He closed his mouth, officially silenced. A bridesmaid had been bad enough, at least she'd get lost with the rest of the cousins and sisters of the bride.

"Best man," he managed, his smile more of a grimace as he held out his beer in a toast.

Caroline didn't extend her glass.

Clearly, she still hated him. Taking another sip of his beer, he decided that it was for the best that she wouldn't hear him out. They were surrounded by friends and family. People who had been in attendance on that fateful day.

People who had put that terrible event behind them. Just like he should.

Like Caroline seemed to have. Still, he couldn't be sure. And the only thing that would be worse than Tim realizing he still had feelings for Caroline was if Caroline still had feelings for him, too.

"I guess that explains the dress," he said, trying to make light of what was becoming a very alarming situation. Caroline was going to be standing beside the bride, at the altar, directly in Tim's sightline.

She gave him a look that showed she wasn't amused. "You happened to walk in on me at a very bad time."

He struggled to hide his smile as the image of her filled his mind. In the past, he'd always made a point of not staring at Caroline, but in this instance, she'd made it downright impossible.

"But the dress is the least of my concerns," Caroline said airily.

Lucas's chest tightened but he tried to keep his tone casual. "Oh? What's on your mind?"

Caroline seemed to hesitate for a moment but then she sighed. Turning her head to face him, she lowered her voice to a near whisper. "Correct me if I'm wrong, but it doesn't seem like there's been a lot of planning for this wedding."

Lucas's only experience had been with the wedding that hadn't happened, but he considered this for a moment. The invitations had gone out with a date. They'd been fitted for the suits, and the women, as evidenced by today, were being fitted for their dresses, as well.

"I think Hillary is handling most of that," Lucas finally

replied. They both knew that Caroline had planned every detail of her wedding to Tim—and it had been beautiful.

Or it would have been.

"Is she, though?" Caroline looked skeptical. "I'm not so sure. She seemed..."

Lucas frowned deeply. He didn't like the uneasy feeling that stirred in his gut. "Seemed what?"

Caroline glanced across the table and then shrugged. "Never mind."

But Lucas certainly did mind. A lot, in fact.

"Hillary and Tim seem very happy to me," Lucas said. Then, realizing how insensitive that must have sounded, he started to backpedal, but not before Caroline had tossed him a withering glance.

"I never said otherwise," she said.

"Look, I didn't mean to upset you," Lucas said. "I'm just protecting my brother."

And himself. Because if this wedding didn't happen, and Wallace pulled out of the hotel, then the entire company would go bust and both Lucas and Tim would be out of jobs. And broke.

"Oh, I'm fully aware of how far you'll go to protect your brother." Caroline gave a laugh that showed no amusement.

Seizing the opportunity, Lucas said, "About that—"

But Caroline's look turned hard. "I'm just saying what I saw and heard. And from what I understand, there isn't much planned other than a venue, cake, and attire. And it makes me wonder why. That's all."

"Are you implying that you don't think there will be a wedding?" Lucas's mouth felt dry and he reached for his beer, barely tasting it. Out of desperation, he asked, "Or are you just hoping there won't be a wedding?"

"Excuse me?" Caroline shot back.

"I wouldn't blame you if a part of you did hope that history would repeat itself, is all I'm saying."

Caroline scoffed. "Hillary isn't just my cousin, she was one of my best friends growing up. She was there for me for everything, including..." She stopped to take a sip of her drink, then took a long breath, closing her eyes for a moment. "I would never, ever wish the kind of pain that Tim caused me onto anyone, especially someone I care about."

Lucas nodded, taking in the words, the emotion, hoping that she meant what she said and that she wasn't still hung up on his brother.

"I can tell you don't believe me," she said, staring at him.

Lucas shifted a little in his chair, uncomfortable with the way her blue eyes were fixed on his, the way her pretty pink mouth pouted ever so slightly.

"I want to believe you," he said honestly. "But after what happened—"

How could Caroline wish Tim happiness? She must despise him.

She must despise them both.

"What happened was three years ago," Caroline said firmly. "Do you really think I'm not over it yet?"

He couldn't respond, because he couldn't be sure. But oh, he wished he could be.

"I'm an event planner," Caroline said. "I own a successful event-planning business."

She paused only long enough for him to give her an appraising look. He wasn't surprised that she'd made something of herself. She'd always been a smart, responsible woman. She hadn't bailed on the wedding she'd so carefully planned, after all.

"I'm happy for Hillary," Caroline went on. "Happy that she's happy. And to prove it, I'm going to volunteer my services to help make this the wedding of her dreams. By the time I'm through with it, she's going to have the most beautiful wedding day that any girl could ever dream of. Because that's what she deserves."

Lucas felt momentarily ashamed of the direction this conversation had taken. "For what it's worth, that's what you deserved, too."

The defiance in her face softened for one telling moment before she lifted her chin.

"Then it looks like I have a wedding to plan," she said. "Unless you object, of course."

He stared at her for a moment before giving a quick shake of the head. He didn't know if he'd just made the biggest mistake of his life, or if he was as desperate as he suddenly felt, but no one in this room knew the bride—or his brother—as well as Caroline did, and if she sensed that there was trouble, then there probably was.

And if she was willing to help, then he was willing to take it.

Even from her of all people.

Five

The next morning, Caroline called Hillary and arranged to meet her for her lunch break. Hillary still held the same position she had before Caroline left town, at the Historical Society not far from the center of town. Armed with a takeout bag from Sweet Harmony and her laptop, Caroline walked through town feeling freer than she had the day before when she was still trying to dodge Tim.

She'd gotten through the worst of it. Surely it could be easier from here on out?

Caroline hurried up the steps of one of the oldest houses in Harmony Cove, a faded cedar Colonial-style home that once belonged to a sea captain and was now a stopping point for tourists looking to learn more about the town's history.

The original pine floorboards creaked under her feet as she walked past glass cases of artifacts collected from some of the founding families, everything from old journals to ship logs, silver tea sets that came over from England with early settlers to children's toys and dolls in ragged and fragile condition. The smell of the house was a cross between old books, worn wood, and, admittedly, dust.

Unable to stop herself, she sneezed. Then sneezed again. By the time Hillary came out of her office, Caroline's eyes were watering.

"Oh, no!" Hillary's face was one of panic as she hurried down the hallway to where Caroline sat on a bench in the front hallway at the base of the stairway, clutching one of the tissues she always had in her purse for emotional clients. "Did something happen? Was it…Tim?"

Caroline frowned at her cousin as she approached, wondering why Hillary would jump to such a conclusion unless she thought that Caroline still wasn't over him.

"No, of course not," she said, standing and seeing a look of relief pass over her cousin's face. "It's the dust. I don't know how you can stand working here!"

"It's a good job," Hillary said, although she didn't sound convincing. History had never been her favorite subject in school, and with her fine arts degree, Caroline had always thought her cousin would have a more creative career. She was forever pressing flowers as a child, doodling in the margins of her notebooks, or experimenting with new clothing styles on the hand-me-down sewing machine from her mother's store.

Still, this place was full of antiques, and she supposed that it let Hillary's imagination roam, albeit it to the past, where it reached its limitations, rather than taking flight, as she had once hoped it would.

"Can we sit outside on a bench?" Caroline asked, eager to get outside into the warm sunshine or, better yet, maybe steal away to the waterfront for a bit. She held up the paper bag from the café. "I brought sandwiches. Turkey on pretzel bread, your favorite."

Hillary checked her watch. "Let's walk to the bay." She linked Caroline's arm and they quickly left the building and crossed the street. The public beach was just a few blocks away, and already the sound of the waves could be heard. When they reached the sand, they both slipped off their shoes, letting them dangle from their fingertips. Caroline let the salty breeze hit her face as she craned her neck up toward the sun.

"I've missed this," she sighed as they settled on a weatherworn picnic table, feeling a thrill of victory that they'd managed to grab it. Summer was in bloom now, and with the weekend approaching, the beach was full of early visitors eager to make the most of the good weather, and young children who were already out of school. The water, Caroline knew from experience, would be cold, but that just added to the shrieks of delight she heard in the distance.

Smiling, she set the two sandwiches on the table—both turkey with arugula and aged white cheddar, both of their favorites, at least it was the last time she'd been here.

She supposed that this might have changed like so many things had in the past three years.

"Your mother makes the best sandwiches," Hillary commented. "She must be happy to have you back."

"She seems happy," Caroline said, even though she wasn't so sure how anyone in her family could be right now. When she'd stopped at the café to pick up the order, her mother had been humming in the kitchen. Humming! Worse, humming with a funny smile on her face.

Caroline had made the decision then and there that it wasn't the best time to talk to her mother about the...separation.

But days had passed, and she wasn't sure there would ever be a right time. She'd come home early from drinks last night but her mother's bedroom light was already out when she'd tiptoed up the stairs.

"I suppose you've heard about my parents," Caroline said as they unwrapped their lunch.

Hillary winced and nodded her head. "No one was as surprised as I was. They always seemed so perfect. Like something out of a fairy tale."

It was true, and not because Hillary grew up without a dad and idealized Caroline's parents' marriage. Sharon and Mitch Baker were the type of couple who seemed forever in love. They were the type who did have a twenty-fifth wedding anniversary party—and the entire town came out to celebrate it in the backyard of their family home. There was a big spread of food, all prepared by Caroline's mother, and a huge cake made by Aunt Kathy, of course. Wine flowed and impromptu speeches were given. There was a kiss and everyone cheered. People danced under strings of lights and stayed until dawn. Caroline had fallen asleep in Tim's arms on the back porch swing after too many glasses of champagne. It had been her twenty-second birthday, and Kathy had been thoughtful enough to bake a second cake for her, too. A dual celebration. A party to end all parties.

It was a night she would never forget. A perfect party. A perfect couple.

But it was all just an illusion.

"I can't believe it," Caroline said to Hillary, shaking her head, knowing that she should believe it, because people broke up all the time, and that she herself didn't believe in love. But she believed in her parents. And she couldn't bring herself to let go of the idea of them just yet. "Do you know what happened?"

Hillary shook her head. "Your parents have been quiet about it."

"Well, there is nothing quiet about the pink highlights in my mother's hair," Caroline remarked, and Hillary tossed her head back and laughed.

Caroline grinned. It felt like old times. It felt good.

And despite how unsettled she felt at seeing her mother looking so different, at feeling like everything was so different, right now, she felt like everything was still very much the same.

"Your mom went through a bit of a thing," Hillary explained. "I'm afraid that my mother might have taken advantage of your mother's change in station. Aunt Sharon was feeling vulnerable and my mother needed more business. Before Sharon could blink an eye, she had a whole new wardrobe and my mother had a sidekick. They must have hit every bar on the Cape by March. They were regulars at a few of them."

"*My* mother?" Caroline gaped.

Hillary tittered nervously. "They even did karaoke a few times in Hyannis."

"No!"

"Yes." Hillary nodded seriously. "If you catch my mother on the right day, she'll show you the video she took. But don't tell your mother. It's a secret."

Caroline clasped a hand to her mouth. Her mother would be mortified to learn this, and only a sister would hold on to such a video, to be pulled out later, as blackmail, or just for some good old-fashioned fun.

"I think your mother eventually got tired of the whole scene," Hillary said. Then, with a sigh, she added, "I wish my mother would."

Caroline felt her heart tug, and she set a hand on her cousin's. She knew all too well that this was a touchy subject. It seemed that it was the story without an ending—or not a happy one, at least. Aunt Sandra was forever looking for a man in all the wrong places, namely bars. Sometimes she even found one, but they never stuck around for long. She was lonely, but she never gave up hope. Most women, especially Caroline, would have by now.

"I've missed this," Hillary said, giving Caroline a long look. "You and me. I worried that I'd never see you again. I started to think that you'd never come back to town. Especially now."

Caroline hadn't intended to come back, at least not anytime soon. She'd gotten comfortable hiding out in Philadelphia, and the more time she stayed away, the easier it became.

And the longer she was on the Cape, the more difficult it was to think of leaving again.

Caroline looked at Hillary. She knew that there was no

dodging the topic forever. It was awkward, and the sooner they discussed it, the sooner they could get on to the reason for this lunch.

"I *was* surprised that you never told me you were dating Tim," Caroline said as she kept her eyes on the sandwich she was unwrapping. She spread the wax paper out as a makeshift plate, her stomach grumbling at the smell of the fresh bread that she knew Molly had baked that morning. "We talked on the phone every couple of months."

Or they did, until the calls between less frequent. At the time, Caroline hadn't thought much of it. She knew how busy she was with her business. She knew that Hillary's job could be demanding at times, too.

She had no reason to think it was because Hillary had met someone. And especially not that the person was Tim.

"How did it come about?" she asked, partly out of curiosity, partly because she was still trying to understand why someone she'd loved and thought she could trust would do what he did.

"Oh, it just sort of happened." Hillary shrugged and then took a big bite of her sandwich. "We saw each other at a holiday party. You know how the Historical Society has one every year. Tim was there, and I hadn't seen him for a while. And last time I had, I was rightfully mad at him for the way he'd treated you. But he said he understood if I didn't want to talk to him."

"He said that?" Caroline's radar was up. It should have been up years ago when he was always going out with friends, staying out later and later, saying he hadn't seen her texts or heard her calls, but well, hindsight and all that.

Hillary nodded. "He seemed really sincere. Like he knew he'd been a jerk. He'd been in Boston since, you know...but he came back to start working on the hotel project with Lucas, not too long after the brothers took over their dad's company. We ran into each other at the Lighthouse Grill a week later, then again at the coffee shop. He invited me for a drink, and by then I didn't see a reason to say no."

She looked at Caroline guiltily.

"It felt good, to feel seen. Noticed. It had been so long since I'd dated anyone, and well, I guess you could say that I'd fallen into a rut. My job is great but it's hardly my passion. All of our other friends from school have moved away. My friends from college are spread out on the coast. And you had moved away. And..."

"I understand," Caroline said, which was true, partly. Hillary's world was small here, and not in a way that she found satisfying. And Tim...Tim could be very charming. "But what I don't understand is why this all happened so soon. I mean, you just started dating. An engagement is one thing, but a wedding?"

Hillary looked at her for a long time until Caroline finally understood.

Hillary hadn't forgotten that day. Not the tears. Not the heartache. She'd witnessed it firsthand—and she was afraid that it would happen to her.

And she was afraid that if she waited to have the wedding, it would just give Tim more time to change his mind.

Caroline opened her mouth and then closed it again, wanting to say so many things, but knowing that her role right now was to support her cousin's decision—and hope for a better outcome than she'd experienced.

"Your wedding is a week away. It doesn't sound like you have all your plans cemented yet," she commented.

Hillary cringed. "I know. It's just that Tim assumed that I'd handle it all. Like—"

"Like I did?" Caroline finished. She had asked for Tim's input at the beginning only to learn quickly that he didn't have any interest in the details. She'd even taken it upon herself to supply him with a short (very short) list of honeymoon destinations, and when they decided together where they wanted to go, she booked the flights and accommodations, too, with Tim's credit card.

But then, she'd known Tim for a decade by then. Hillary had really known Tim intimately (oh, that felt so strange) for only a matter of months.

"It's a short time frame, like you said, and I guess once I started planning everything, I didn't realize just how much there was to do," Hillary continued, setting down her sandwich. "My mother's already making all the bridesmaid dresses, and the wedding dress is her gift to me. She's been working until the middle of the night to get everything ready in time while running the store, and between you and me, I'm kicking myself that we have such a big family."

Caroline managed to grin. She'd always loved that between her three sisters and her six local cousins, they were ten women strong. Twelve if you counted their uncle's two girls, who lived in New York. A perfect dozen. A dirty dozen to hear some tell it, especially when they got into mischief in their younger days.

"My mother's store hasn't been doing well," Hillary said, darting her eyes around the beach to kids playing frisbee or splashing in the water, couples strolling hand in hand, stopping only to pick up a shell.

It was a sacred time for locals, when the weather was warm, but the town wasn't yet overwhelmed by day-trippers or weekenders. Caroline supposed that in some ways, she had picked the perfect time to visit.

"Is Tim contributing?" It wasn't a secret that the Reynoldses had money.

"Oh…" Hillary wrinkled her nose. "It's tradition for the bride and all, and…"

And she didn't want to upset the applecart, as the saying went. Alarm bells went off, but Caroline kept her worries to herself.

"You can work out something on a budget," she suggested instead. "And I can help you with that."

Hillary's eyes filled with tears. "You would? You will?"

Caroline nodded firmly, more than certain that helping plan this wedding was the right thing to do—not just to prove her point to Lucas but to help her cousin have the day that she deserved.

That they both did, she thought, remembering Lucas's words.

Had it been a moment of kindness? She let that thought go as soon it entered her mind. Lucas was as selfishly motivated as his father. And his brother. He was a Reynolds, after all.

"Why don't you tell me what you have so far, and then we can figure out the rest?" Caroline listened while Hillary gave a vague and slightly dispassionate rundown of the few things she'd secured, mostly thanks to the help of family: the cake from their aunt Kathy's bakery and the rehearsal dinner at Sweet Harmony.

"Kayla offered to do the photos," she added, picking at her sandwich.

That still left music, seating, and a few more important items.

"What about flowers?" Caroline asked. An easy, obvious task.

"I thought that I could pick some from the garden," Hillary said, looking doubtful. "If there's enough to go around..."

No one made a better daisy chain than Hillary, but this was her wedding day she was talking about, and the bride shouldn't be running around stuffing flowers into vases when she was supposed to be getting ready. Perhaps her sisters could at least offer to take on the task, but Caroline hoped to do one better and speak to the local florist about placing an order.

"What does Tim say about all of this?" Caroline was genuinely curious.

"I haven't mentioned any specifics to him." Hillary bit into her sandwich and looked out over the water.

Hm. Caroline was beginning to wonder just what Hillary and Tim did talk about, but that was a problem for another day. She could tell by the glum expression on Hillary's face that this was hardly turning out to be the wedding she'd imagined when they were little girls, dreaming about their futures in the tree house in Caroline's yard.

Hillary glanced back at her. "I...didn't want to worry him with the details. And...I know I'll figure it all out."

Would she? This didn't seem like the Hillary that Caroline knew, and she wanted to pry, to ask what was really going on, but then Hillary lit up with a bright smile, and said, "But now I don't have to worry! I have you helping me!"

"You do," Caroline confirmed. "I'll come up with a plan this afternoon and then we can talk about it more this evening. I know how to cut corners, and I'm sure I can pull a few strings with some vendors around here."

Though on such short notice, she wasn't so sure.

"You'd do that?" Hillary stood up and came around the table to hug her.

"It's my gift to you," Caroline said, realizing with shame that since she hadn't planned to attend this wedding, she hadn't thought to buy a gift.

"No, you being here is a gift to me," Hillary said, giving her another squeeze. "First my maid of honor. Now this. Oh, Caroline. I thought you'd never speak to me again. You're a good person. Such a good person."

But not good enough for Tim, she couldn't help but think.

She could only hope that the same wasn't true for Hillary.

∼

Caroline decided to go back to the café to collect her thoughts, knowing that the crowd would have thinned since the lunch rush. She found a table near the window, gave a wave to Molly who stood behind the counter, and dropped into a chair.

No flowers. No food for the actual wedding reception. Had Hillary seriously mentioned the word *potluck* before she'd left her at the stoop of the Historical Society? Caroline had a dozen unanswered questions and concerns but only one thing was for certain right now: time was not on their side. And the budget didn't help.

Hillary had tossed out a number, one that would barely cover a children's birthday party, much less a catered event for seventy people. But when Caroline had suggested she ask Tim to pitch in, Hillary had clammed up, insisting that he was financially strapped with the new hotel and that she didn't want to bother him with this so close to the wedding.

If Caroline were a betting woman, she'd say that Hillary was afraid of handing Tim an easy excuse to call the whole thing off.

With a sigh, she pulled out her notebook and looked at the notes she'd taken, adding a few ideas of her own that she'd run by Hillary later. She was sure that if she asked her mother or Molly, they would agree to cater the reception, but she also knew that they were already hosting the rehearsal dinner—no doubt as a gift.

She didn't know how long she had been sitting there when she felt the pull of someone's stare from across the room, and sure enough, there near the counter was none other than Lucas.

It would seem that, unlike his brother, Lucas had no shame when it came to frequenting her family's business.

Either that, or he couldn't resist her mother's clam chowder, which was entirely possible.

Either way, he didn't deserve them.

Caroline felt her mood wither when she realized that instead of heading out the door, Lucas was making his way over to her table. She quickly spread out her notepad and pulled her laptop from her bag, hoping to deter him from sitting down, but he only paused, took in the scene, and then pulled out the chair.

"Can I help you with something?" she asked, keeping her tone as neutral as possible when what she really wanted to tell him was that he'd said enough for one lifetime.

"Are these the plans for the wedding?" he asked, reaching into the take-out bag and removing a chicken sandwich on her mother's signature pesto bread.

"They are," she said. "Would you like to see?" She turned the notebook to face him, eager to hear his thoughts, considering that Tim wasn't sharing any.

Lucas took his time reading over her notes and then gave her a funny look. "You've put a lot of work into this."

"It's what I do," she said with a shrug. No need to mention that the only wedding she'd planned other than the one last week had been her own. "Event planning was a natural transition after working at the Bayview Inn."

"Oh, that's right." He nodded, giving her a thoughtful look. "You worked for your aunt."

She nodded, lest she roll her eyes. Of course he'd forgotten what she'd done for a living all through her twenties if he'd ever known at all.

"The inn always has special events." She tipped her head. "I hear that you're opening a hotel in town."

Lucas fought off a grin as he nodded, and Caroline was momentarily thrown off guard. It was, perhaps, the first time Lucas Reynolds had actually looked…happy.

"We just broke ground. It won't be anything like the Bayview Inn," he said quickly. "But we don't aim to compete. That inn is a local treasure. Our hotel will be on a bigger scale. A resort experience."

Caroline raised her eyebrows. She couldn't help but be impressed. "I thought Reynolds Properties developed office properties."

"The market has changed," Lucas said with a shrug.

"So you're back in town to stay?" she hedged when what she really wanted to know were Tim's long-term plans and how they might impact her cousin—and maybe herself.

Lucas hesitated long enough for her pulse to skip. "That's the hope." He went back to the notes she'd made and then looked at her. "What about you? How long are you in town for?"

Her ticket was open-ended, and she'd intended to stay only long enough to make sure that her family was okay, preferably heading out before the big wedding day. Once again, plans had changed for her, and her to-do list had no control over any of it.

She had nothing waiting for her in Philadelphia, but she would never get her business on track by staying away, either.

"I'm here until next Sunday," she said, thinking that by the day after the wedding, she'd likely be very ready to get back to her quiet life.

Her lonely life.

Lucas nodded and looked over her notes again. "You have some good ideas here. I have to say that I'm impressed."

"You sound surprised," she said, yanking her notebook back and closing it firmly.

"I am surprised," he said.

"Surprised that my ideas are good or surprised that I had any at all?" she asked calmly.

"I guess both?"

She raised an eyebrow at him. Two points for honesty, she supposed, though he'd never been lacking in that area, had he? Frank to the point of rude, really.

"I mean, I wasn't sure you meant it when you said that you'd help," he said, reddening a little in the cheeks.

"I'm a person of my word," she said coldly. "I, unlike some, have integrity." She managed a small smile.

That silenced him.

"Like I said last night, my only goal is to make sure that Hillary gets to have the wedding I never did." She paused for a moment, pushing back the emotion that filled her chest. The disappointment was still there, along with the memory of the anticipation that had led up to what was supposed to be the first day of the rest of her life and instead was the last day of her relationship. "If I can help make that happen by lending my professional services, then I'm going to do that."

Lucas looked at her thoughtfully for a moment, the sandwich momentarily forgotten. "That's really nice of you."

"I'm a nice person," Caroline said simply. Not that he'd

ever taken the time to notice before. "And there obviously isn't much time to pull this together."

"What can I do to help?" Lucas blurted, and now Caroline was the one to stare carefully at him. He looked sincere. And he sounded genuine. But why did he suddenly care about how this wedding turned out when he was all too happy to watch hers fail?

"I can manage this," she assured him. "It's what I do every day." Or at least some days, when she had an actual client. "The only sticking point is the budget."

"Not a problem," Lucas said, leaning back in his chair. "Consider it covered."

Caroline blinked at him, trying to process what he'd just suggested. Sure, Lucas Reynolds came from the Reynolds fortune, but this sudden burst of generosity still came as a surprise. Where had this support been for her wedding?

"Are you offering to pay for the wedding?" she clarified.

Lucas nodded. "Don't worry Hillary or her family by telling them so, though. Or Tim," he added quickly, and, if Caroline didn't know better, a little urgently.

"These types of things can get expensive," Caroline warned him, lest he, like his brother, make a promise he wasn't going to keep. "And aren't you in the process of building a resort?"

"Let me worry about my business affairs," he told her. "Now, what do we still need for the wedding?"

She opened her notebook again, picking a few items from her list. "Food for the reception. Flowers for the ceremony. Centerpieces." She could get creative with those, especially at the beach. They didn't need to be flowers, though flowers would be lovely, and Hillary did love them so.

Lucas absorbed this information but then nodded. "Come to me with any questions. I trust you to get a good deal where you can."

Trust. That was certainly a big word. And not a sentiment that she shared.

"Why are you doing this?" she asked, closing her notebook to narrow her eyes on him.

Lucas pulled in a breath and then, after a beat, released it. "Tim can be a little too hands-off when it comes to details and plans, whereas I enjoy managing a big project. And like you said, Hillary deserves a nice wedding. And for what it's worth, so did you, Caroline."

He pushed back his chair and stood, leaving her to absorb what he'd just said as he slipped out the door. She didn't know which part was more shocking, that he was willing to foot the bill for this entire wedding or that he'd just maybe admitted to regretting what had happened at her own wedding.

"Caroline?" Her mother wove through the maze of tables and glanced out the window with a worried look before slipping into the chair that Lucas had just vacated. "I saw you talking to Lucas. Is everything okay?"

"Just discussing wedding plans since I've offered to help Hillary..."

Caroline sat a little straighter, about to launch into the dreaded conversation, when her mother leaned in closely and nearly whispered, "Then you're just the person I should be talking to! There will be another guest to add to your list."

"Oh?" Caroline clicked her pen and poised it over her notebook.

Her mother smiled broadly. "I have a date."

And just like that, all hope Caroline held for getting through to her mother vanished. She stared at the woman across from her, whose green eyes gleamed in a way that she hadn't seen in years. Maybe it was the pink streaks in her otherwise graying blond hair that brought out the natural blush in her cheeks, or maybe it was the warm sunlight pouring in through the window, but right now her mother looked younger somehow, and happier than she had in a long time.

When was it that she'd stopped being happy? Caroline thought sadly. And why was it that Caroline had never noticed until now?

"A date?" Caroline swallowed hard, fighting back the tears that threatened to fall when she thought of her father, reassuring her that everything would be okay when it no longer felt like that was possible at all. She wanted to press, to ask what went wrong between them, to understand how someone could love someone one day and not the next.

But she also knew that there was only one right thing to say, much as there was with Hillary. "I'm happy for you, Mom."

She just wasn't so sure that this wedding was going to end happily. For anyone.

Six

Lucas hung up the phone with his second biggest investor and sank his head into his hands. It was only eleven in the morning but somehow it felt like it was already six in the evening. His head ached along with his shoulders, and he had half a mind to call it a day and go home—only he still had a budget meeting to schedule and a chef to interview before he could call it quits, and even then, he knew his day wouldn't stop.

Unlike his brother, who was yet to make an appearance at the office today, probably because it was Friday, and Tim was known to start his weekends on Thursdays. Lucas didn't clock out at five, and he didn't have the ability to sit back with a beer and turn off his worries, either.

Someone in the family had to worry, after all, and in the Reynolds household, it had always been Lucas, as far back as he could remember, back when his parents were still married, fighting every spare minute they had. How could Lucas not lose sleep worrying that they'd get a divorce? And when they had, and he and his brother had stayed on the Cape with their mother, his anxiety only mounted, even though his worst fear had already come true. He worried what his mother would say after weekends in the city spent with his father. And he worried when his father got engaged again—quickly, too quickly—and what he should tell his mother about that, or if he should say nothing at all. He'd tried to make life easy for her, getting good grades, being what most would call a "good" kid, and keeping an eye on Tim, whom many would not necessarily call a "good" kid.

Not that Tim was bad, per se. But Tim wasn't concerned —about his parents, about grades, about anything, really. He didn't take life seriously, and his reaction to the stress of their homelife was to have as much fun as he could outside of it.

A skill that Lucas often envied growing up, and, if he was honest with himself, still did some days.

But not today. Tim's wedding was now a little over a week away. They had just broken ground on their first project after taking over the family business, and it was a major development, one that required long hours and didn't leave much room for error.

Was it ambitious? Yes. Was the timing the best? Probably not. But the opportunity might not come along again. Land availability was tight in Harmony Cove, and if it wasn't now it might have been never.

And if Tim decided to walk away from this wedding, he'd be blowing up all their plans with it.

"Tim!" Lucas said when his brother finally came through the door of the trailer half an hour later. They'd set up a temporary camp at the building site so that Lucas could oversee every stage of the development and be available when the architects and contractors needed him, all while managing the corporate office remotely. He'd made the cramped space his home away from home, but Tim bounced in when he saw fit, finding more and more excuses to wine and dine their investors to keep them happy, usually at the nearby country club, always on the company dime, of course, which really meant Lucas's dime.

Some days, when the phone wouldn't stop ringing and his email inbox was piling up, this drove Lucas crazy, but today he was all too happy to ask Tim to court some of their more comfortable relationships—it would take the pressure off potentially losing Wallace Hadley.

Tim dropped his bag behind the small partition that divided their spaces. "You sound surprised that I'm here."

"It is nearly noon," Lucas pointed out.

"Is it?" Tim glanced at his watch. "I have to meet Hillary in half an hour. If you need me earlier, next time just call, bro."

If only it could always be that simple with his brother, Lucas lamented. Ever since they were kids, he'd struggled to count on Tim for anything, and maybe that was because Tim knew that he didn't have to be the responsible sibling when Lucas was playing the part so well.

Wasn't Lucas the one to make sure Tim still got dinner on the nights his parents were too busy fighting to think about something as trivial as cooking a meal? Wasn't it Lucas who made sure that Tim packed everything he'd need for a weekend at their dad's because his mother wanted nothing to do with the mere thought of it?

"Steve Owens is breathing down my neck about the signature restaurant," Lucas told Tim. They'd pitched the project as not just being a high-end resort, but one that would come with a celebrity chef, one that would make the hotel stand out from its counterparts, that would garner attention from vacationers on the eastern seaboard. Lucas had interviewed three well-known chefs in New York and two in Boston, but none of them were a match for the kind of atmosphere he envisioned.

"Want me to invite him to golf and talk him down?" Tim said. Unlike Wallace, Steve had been brought in by Tim, and the two had an easy, casual relationship. The one time the three of them had gone to dinner, Lucas had felt awkward while the two other men knocked back beers and laughed about college shenanigans when Lucas had hoped they'd discuss his plans for the hotel.

"Do you even have time?" Lucas asked, glancing at the calendar on his desk, the one that showed Tim's wedding day in thick black ink. Another week was scratched off for a honeymoon, the location of which even he didn't know.

Caroline's words came back to him now, making his gut stir with unease.

Tim shrugged to show that he wasn't concerned. "Hillary's got the wedding under control."

Was this what Tim thought or what Hillary would have him believe? Lucas thought of what Caroline had said and became suspicious.

Tim grinned and leaned back in his chair. "All I have to do is show up."

Lucas stared at his brother for a hard second, wondering

if that was a slip of the tongue or a lame attempt at a joke. Judging from the ruddiness of Tim's complexion as he straightened in his chair, he assumed that his brother realized the meaning of his words.

And that he was probably thinking about his last wedding. And Caroline.

"Speaking of that," Lucas said carefully. "I was surprised to see that Caroline was back. Did you know she was going to be in the wedding party?"

He held his breath, knowing that Tim wasn't one to open up any more than Lucas was, but hoping that he'd at least quell his concerns about any lingering feelings.

"Hillary's really happy that Caroline agreed to be her maid of honor," Tim said without any emotion. "And if Hillary's happy, then I'm happy."

Only Tim didn't look happy. And he wasn't acting like a man who was about to marry the love of his life in a week, either.

But then, he hadn't been acting like a man about to marry the love of his life in the months and even years leading up to his wedding to Caroline if his late-night activities said anything.

And look how that had turned out.

"I don't think you ever told me your plans for the honeymoon." Lucas hoped his tone sounded more casual than he felt.

He waited for Tim to announce a grand destination—somewhere expensive and difficult to get to. In other words, an irresponsible choice. But instead, Tim laced his fingers over the back of his head and said pensively, "You know, I'm still figuring that out."

Lucas gaped at his brother as his heart started to pound. He should have known. This was Tim, for crying out loud. Tim never thought to buy either of his parents a Christmas or birthday gift, but always grinned and said he'd go in on whatever Lucas picked out. Just recently, Tim had forgotten Mother's Day and had asked Lucas to tell their mother that he was sick, even though Lucas knew darn well he was on the sixteenth hole at the club. Tim was always making a mess, and Lucas was always picking up after him.

But not this time.

There would be a wedding. He had too much at stake for there not to be one.

"You haven't planned it yet?" He struggled to keep his voice from rising but his heart pounded in his rib cage. "But won't Hillary need to request time off from work? And what about flights and hotels?"

Tim just shrugged. "I'm sure that Hillary has requested the time off. And there are plenty of hotels in this world."

Like Lucas needed the reminder.

Turning away from his brother, he studied the rendering of the project that he kept pinned to the wall. He felt his stomach knot at the possibility of the hotel failing. Deep down, he knew that wasn't completely impossible. Accommodations were booked out on the Cape well before the start of the summer season, sometimes even a year in advance. But success wasn't just about filling rooms. It was about giving the guests the experience they were promising.

One that he at least believed in.

"Hey, have we figured out what to do about the location of the pool?" Tim asked a few minutes later. He pointed to his computer screen. "Speaking of Steve, he just emailed to ask where we stand with the permit for that."

Another problem yet to be resolved. And if Steve was worried, then that meant the other investors weren't far behind.

"We should know within a few days," Lucas said.

"And if we don't get approved to put it on the waterfront?" Tim asked the question that everyone involved in the project was wondering—and worrying about.

Lucas looked at the rendering again, the one that showed the hotel as it should be—but how often did anything go as planned?

"We'll worry about that later," Lucas said tersely. At least there was an alternate plan for the pool's location. There was no backup for Tim failing to show up for his wedding. "For now, we keep moving forward and hope it all works out."

That's all he could do, and just like when he was younger, and his parents were screaming until the crystal chandelier in the dining room shook, he didn't like that feeling.

Of being helpless. But not, he told himself, without hope.

"I'll set up a round of golf tomorrow and reassure him that everything is going to plan," Tim said.

If only Lucas could believe that was true. "Hey, why don't you invite him to the wedding while you're at it?"

The words landed with silence. Tim's brow knitted for a moment, enough time for Lucas to regret making the suggestion. But Tim respected Steve. He wouldn't want to let him down.

"Sure, okay." A moment later, Tim was already laughing with Steve, chatting about sports and golf and who knew what else, seemingly without a care in the world. Lucas pulled up Wallace's email and began drafting an update. Wallace, the family guy. Wallace with his five kids, eleven grandkids, and a wife of thirty years.

And a front-row seat at Tim's wedding.

Caroline was both satisfied and more than a little anxious about everything that still needed to be done for the wedding, but still, she had a list and that alone was armor. Comfort. A reassurance that at least some things in this world were within her control.

She and Hillary had worked on wedding plans for hours the night before over a bottle of sauvignon blanc and leftovers Caroline's mother had brought back from the café, and while she knew what needed to be tackled, she still wasn't sure if she could pull it off on such a short timeline.

Or if Lucas had been serious about his offer.

Deciding that there was only one way to find out, and secure in the knowledge that Hillary was lunching with Tim, she parked her old yellow bicycle at the foot of the beach trail that stopped just short of the construction site and, according to the big sign that was angled to face both the beach and the nearby street, the future family-friendly resort. The framing had only just begun, but already she could tell that the project would be expansive and impressive, meaning that despite the shift from office properties to hotels, not much had changed with the Reynolds family. They'd always been a prominent fixture in town; Mrs. Reynolds had kept the large family home with coveted views of the Atlantic, and Caroline knew from her few short visits to Boston with Tim that Mr. Reynolds lived even larger with a large townhome in Beacon Hill and a "cottage" in Newport. They were successful, with much to show for it.

Except love.

And maybe, Caroline thought, thinking of Lucas, happiness.

The sea breeze blew her hair, and she gathered it back into a ponytail before it grew tangled. She collected her notebook from the rattan basket attached to her handlebars and then took her time walking along the sandy path toward the trailer with the company's logo displayed prominently on its side. Construction workers came and went, and the squawking of seagulls was interrupted by the pounding of nails and the sound of power tools. Hedging her bets that Lucas was tucked safely inside the trailer rather than donning a hard hat, she knocked twice on the door, loudly, so she had a chance of being heard over the noise.

"Come in!" a voice barked, making Caroline jump.

It wasn't exactly the most welcoming invitation, but still, she reached for the handle and yanked it open, coming face-to-face with Lucas, who was sitting behind a desk.

When he saw her, the anger left his face, and if she didn't know better, she'd say he almost looked apologetic.

"Expecting someone else?" she asked, stepping inside the cramped but well-lit space.

"I've been interrupted all day with one problem or another," he said, shaking his head.

"I didn't meet to bother you," Caroline started, turning to go.

"No, it's fine. I could use a break." Lucas actually grinned at her, and Caroline felt unnerved for a moment.

Up until now, she wasn't even sure the man had a full set of teeth, though, given his rigid habits, she had to assume he did and that they were professionally cleaned with a standing appointment every six months on the dot.

But what really bothered her was that his smile was nice. More than nice. It lifted his features, crinkling the corners of his dark eyes and making them come to life in a way that almost made him seem...approachable. Likeable even.

But she couldn't like Lucas. Not in any sense. Not even if he had made such a generous offer yesterday.

Not wanting to jump onto that topic just yet, she decided to feel him out.

"That's some project you have going on out there."

Lucas nodded, his warm expression turning anxious again. "It's hard to believe it will ever be finished by the looks of it."

"And what will it look like when it's complete?" Caroline asked, genuinely curious. Harmony Cove was a small town, and up until now, it had catered to small inns, B&Bs, and cottage rentals. A resort like this would be a first for their town, and she wondered if it would change it for the better or the worse.

"I can show you the rendering, if you'd like?" Lucas didn't wait for her to reply to wave her over to his desk, where a large colored drawing was pinned to the wall.

"Wow," Caroline said, feeling genuinely impressed. It was a large building, but one that was full of character, with architecture similar to some of her favorite houses in town. The structure would be cedar shingled with white trim, wrapped with a huge porch that faced the bay. On each site, there was a large gabled room, and one side of the building showed expansive gardens, and on the other a large pool, with tennis courts beyond it.

"What's that?" Caroline asked, pointing to a little stand near the pool's waterslide.

"That is a snow cone machine." Lucas sounded excited. "The kids will love it, and it will hardly cost the hotel anything. Shaved ice. A little sugar syrup. It's the little things like this that will keep the kids wanting to come back—meaning the adults, too."

For someone who didn't have kids, Caroline was surprisingly impressed that Lucas, who never seemed to have been much of a kid himself, would think of such a thing.

Unless...

"Tim's idea?" she asked. If there was one thing Tim *could* be counted on, it was for a good time.

Lucas glanced at her, frowning briefly. "Mine. I handle the business end. Tim's the rainmaker."

Her brows shot up before she could hide her surprise.

"When we used to visit my dad in Boston, he was usually working, even on weekends," Lucas explained. "Most of the time we just sat around the house, bored. But there was this snow cone cart at the park in the summertime, and no matter how busy my father was, he always made sure that he took us over there for a treat." Lucas's expression turned wistful. "We used to sit on a park bench, and my dad would always tell us to eat it before it melted, especially on hot days, but I always tried to make mine last as long as I could."

"To savor the taste?" Caroline couldn't help but grin at the strangely sweet memory he was sharing.

Lucas's expression clouded. "Because I knew when I was finished, he'd go straight back to the office."

He turned abruptly, forcing his attention back to the rendering, his jaw pulsing when she studied his profile, struggling for what to say. Tim rarely mentioned his father, and when he did, he didn't seem to have much emotion toward the man.

But then, Tim didn't have much emotion toward her, either, as it had turned out.

"Well, it's a really good idea," she told Lucas, giving praise where it was due. Then, because she was eager to change the topic, she said, "What else do you have planned?"

She listened as he told her about the beach chair service and the heated pool, the cabanas that people could rent for the day, and the complimentary bikes they could use to ride into town. His voice rose with excitement as he gestured to each point on the rendering, but then he stood and said, "If you have time, I could show you."

Caroline didn't have much time if she wanted to get this wedding planned, but considering that Lucas may or may not be handling the tab, she nodded. It wouldn't kill her to spend a little time with the man—even if he had delivered the most hurtful words that haunted her to this day.

They stepped outside into the warm sunshine, and Caroline breathed in the salty air.

"I love the smell of the ocean, don't you?" she said, her good spirits taking over and bringing her to nearly smile at the man beside her.

"Why do you think I moved back to the Cape?" Lucas said as he led her up the path to the construction site.

"I assumed it was for work," Caroline admitted. Even growing up, Lucas always had his head in a textbook and chose schoolwork over fun.

His grin was wry. "Work brought me back here. When I saw the opportunity, I couldn't let it pass me by. Boston is a different pace, and life there was always about different priorities, mainly revolving around my father's wishes, but this is what I always wanted to do. Give people the full Harmony Cove experience."

"At least an idyllic one," Caroline observed, thinking of all the plans he'd described.

"And why shouldn't it be?" Lucas countered with a good-natured shrug. "Vacation is an escape from the real world and all its troubles. And Harmony Cove is the perfect backdrop."

"It's a beautiful place," she agreed, feeling a twinge of homesickness, even though she was right here, right now.

"It looked more beautiful every time I returned to it. I just hope I can do it justice." Lucas's expression resumed the tense tightness that she'd come to know him for, but it relaxed again as they approached the building site, where the foundation had already been put down. He used his hands to gesture where everything would be positioned, his face relaxing as he described his vision.

"And there, near the gardens, I thought we could have lawn games. Mini golf, croquet, sand bag, that type of thing."

She looked up at him, giving him a funny smile.

He must have caught it because he suddenly looked self-conscious, the little frown appearing between his eyebrows as he stuffed his hands in his pockets and stiffly said, "What is it?"

"Nothing," she said honestly. "It's nice seeing you so excited about this. I guess I just... Well, I guess I never took you for a family man, is all."

As soon as she said it, she wanted to take the words back. It was rude, and maybe even hurtful, but Lucas just shrugged again.

"It's no secret in these parts that I didn't grow up in the most traditional family, and I certainly don't intend to have one of my own, but that doesn't mean I can't make it happen for others. That I can't give them the perfect, *idyllic* experience." He smiled again, looking at her, his eyes crinkling at the corners.

Caroline stared at him for a moment, wondering if he really meant that or if that was just what he told himself. Everyone knew about Tim and Lucas's parents and their public divorce—and their even more public arguments before their separation.

Maybe, she realized, it was what he'd wanted for himself. And now, might be able to have. At long last.

Lucas led her along a beach path, and she walked alongside him, listening as he pointed and explained where everything would be positioned, how there would be a ballroom to use for parties, and a signature restaurant off of the lobby. How he planned to have a brass band play in the lobby bar every weekend.

"If you're going with the theme of yesteryear, then you could have them wear costumes similar to the time period. Even a seersucker suit would go a long way."

Lucas stopped walking to stare at her, and for a moment, Caroline was afraid she'd spoken out of turn. But then Lucas grinned—for the second time that day—and said, "That's a fantastic idea. And not just for the band, but for the entire staff. Thank you."

Caroline blushed. "It's nothing. It's just how my mind works. I think of a theme, and I run with the details."

Which was exactly what she was hoping to do with Hillary's beach wedding. Sand. Shells. Simple flowers, all in creamy white. Even the turquoise bridesmaid dresses would look beautiful with the vision she'd created last night.

Now, if only to execute it.

"About the wedding," she said before she lost her nerve. "Were you serious about paying for it?"

He stared at her blankly. "When I give my word, I mean it."

Caroline was unable to speak, because all she could think of was Tim, and how he had given his word, and failed to keep it.

Lucas must have picked up on her reaction because his

expression softened. "Look, I heard what you said about the wedding and the lack of plans. As much as I hate to say it, I think you're right to be concerned. And if I can help in some way by writing a few checks, then that's what I'll do. This wedding is important to the family. We have some big investors attending. Before I forget, there are two new names to add to the list. Possibly a third by tomorrow, four if he brings a date."

"Ah." And there it was. She should have known that Lucas wasn't doing this out of the goodness of his heart. But for some reason, she felt an ache of disappointment. One that had no place living inside her.

"What do you mean by that?" he asked, frowning.

"Nothing," she said brusquely, lest he change his mind. Though, given the self-serving reasons behind his generosity, she doubted he would. "Besides, don't you think we've both said enough?"

"You think I'm only helping with the wedding because I have VIP guests attending," Lucas commented.

Caroline didn't try to deny it. "Are you telling me it's out of the goodness of your heart?" She could kick herself for ever thinking that such a thing might be true.

Lucas tossed up his hands. "This hotel is important to me. So is my brother. The two just happen to overlap."

Caroline suspected that there was more he wasn't telling her but said nothing about that. "Believe me, I of all people know just how important your brother is to you."

"You're mad at me," he said, and this time she didn't try to stop him. Darn right she was mad at him—and who wouldn't be? "I feel terrible for what Tim did to you. For the record, I didn't agree with him, but then, my brother and I don't agree on much."

"It sure seemed like you had his side that day," Caroline said, hating the hurt that she could hear in her voice. She wondered if Lucas could pick up on it, or if he even cared.

"I had a message to deliver, that was all," he said, holding her gaze, until she was forced to search his eyes, to seek the truth there. And she saw it. The slight pinch of his brows. The frown that pulled at his mouth. "I never wanted to be put in that position."

"Then why agree to it?"

His silence told her she had him there, and he opened his mouth and then closed it again, until she decided that there wasn't anything he could say that would change anything.

"For the sake of *this* wedding, we can let it go," she said, shaking her head. She hadn't come here to dwell on old wounds.

Relief loosened Lucas's features. "I do want this to be a success. And not just because of the guest list," he added. "I mean it."

She stared at him for a moment, wondering if she should believe him.

Because the last time she'd taken a Reynolds man at their word, it had ended with a broken heart.

Seven

The next morning, Caroline met Hillary and Sandra at the Bayside Bakery, where Kathy was waiting for them with a plate of cake samples. Kathy greeted Caroline with a quick hug and a waggle of her eyebrows followed by a wink. Code for *We'll talk later*.

Oh, yes, they would, but the conversation wasn't only about Hillary marrying Tim. If Marcy somehow knew that Caroline would be standing at the altar as the maid of honor, then surely Kathy knew by now, too.

And did she know about her older sister's date? And if so, did she know who the man was, and just how well Sharon knew him?

Caroline hadn't told her own sisters about their mother's announcement yet, but that was only because for the first time since her return to town, their mother had been at home early, insisting on a sit-down dinner with her oldest and youngest daughters. Not wanting to ruin the moment,

Caroline had kept the conversation to neutral and pleasant topics—and in return, no one mentioned the wedding.

But now the wedding was only one week away, and many details were yet to be finalized. The bakery wasn't yet open for business, meaning that they didn't need to worry about pulling Kathy's attention from customers, and Kathy insisted that all of her baking was finished for the morning, thanks to the help of her assistant. Like Caroline's mother, Kathy enlisted the help of one of her daughters, hoping to keep the business in the family for generations to come.

"I have coffee for everyone," Lucy said as she came through the kitchen door, carrying a tray of mugs and a carafe.

Caroline stood to help her cousin, who flashed her a look of appreciation and gave her a huge hug the moment her hands were free. "I can't believe you're back!"

That made two of them. Caroline squeezed Lucy's hand and said, "You'll join us, won't you?"

"I never say no to cake for breakfast." Lucy wasted no time pulling out a chair.

"I always say that the only difference between a muffin and cake is the frosting," Kathy said as she passed around small plates and forks. Going along with the pastel theme of the bakery, each plate was a different color, shape, and even size, an effect that was both charming and functional to hear Kathy tell it; she didn't ever have to worry about replacing a broken dish as none of them matched in the first place.

"This certainly looks like the best breakfast I've ever had," Caroline said as her stomach rumbled happily. As often as she helped clients pick out celebration cakes, or oversaw the delivery of them, she rarely had the chance to taste any herself. "Which flavors do we have here?"

"I took the season into consideration," Kathy began. She pointed to each of the options as she explained their flavoring. "Lemon with blackberry, lemon with raspberry, vanilla with raspberry, and of course you can't go wrong with classic vanilla."

Caroline noted that Kathy hadn't included the flavor of her own wedding cake. She'd selected a vanilla sponge with lemon curd.

While Hillary and Sandra exchanged their preliminary thoughts on the choices, Caroline caught Kathy giving her a discreet wink across the table. She felt her heart warm at the camaraderie, the pain of the past once again fading away, a memory better forgotten and replaced by the reminder that some people were always in her corner.

"Shall we dig in?" Caroline asked because she still had to go the flower shop today *and* find a band, and then there was the rather frightening problem of finding a caterer who would be available in one week's time. Her best bet was a sudden cancelation, which, she knew from personal experience, was entirely possible.

Though not exactly probable.

They each took a small slice of each flavor, Sandra going for seconds on a few while lamenting her lack of a date for her own daughter's wedding, and while Caroline felt the samples were equally delicious, they agreed that it all came down to personal preference.

"You're the bride," Caroline said to Hillary. "You choose."

"But I brought you all here for your input," Hillary said. "I want my guests to be happy, too."

There was a beat of silence. It was a tall order, expecting the groom's ex-fiancée to be happy at his wedding. But still, Caroline was trying her best.

"Yes, but it's *your* wedding," Caroline reminded her cousin, as difficult as it was to say, and as odd as it felt. "And it should be everything that you dreamed it would be."

At least one of them should get the wedding they hoped for.

"In that case, I think I'll go with the lemon raspberry," Hillary said, giving them all a nervous grin. "It's really starting to feel real now. A part of me still doesn't believe it's really happening."

Caroline caught Kathy's eye. Did her aunt sense it, too? That something was amiss here? Or was Kathy, like Caroline, just remembering what happened the last time Tim Reynolds said he was getting married?

Kathy went back to scribbling in her notebook, sharing a few ideas for the size and shape, and then opened a big binder full of photos of wedding cakes. Caroline had to hand it to her aunt, she had a true gift for design, and each cake was executed flawlessly. She paused every few pages for Hillary to remark on what she liked or didn't like about the photograph, and even Caroline couldn't help but get caught up in the beauty of the images until Kathy turned to the next page, and her heart dropped like a stone.

There it was. A round, four-layer, three-tier wedding cake in white fondant, with a trail of pastel fondant flowers winding its way up to the top, where her aunt had expertly re-created Caroline's wedding bouquet out of buttercream. Caroline remembered how she'd felt when she first saw it. How she'd said that it looked too pretty to cut.

Little did she know that it never would be.

Now she wondered what had happened to the cake. When she'd fled the church with her sisters and parents, her aunts and cousins had offered to stay back, Kathy reassuring her that they'd take care of everything.

She couldn't imagine that they'd eaten the dessert. Maybe Kathy had donated it, along with the flowers, to someone who could put it to better use. The senior center would have put both to good use. Or even the nearby hospital.

Kathy quickly turned the page, but not before the damage was done. Lucy and Hillary exchanged a glance, Sandra seemed oblivious as she reached for the last cake sample, even though they'd already decided on the flavor, and Kathy talked quickly as she flipped to the next photograph, one that Hillary seemed to like. Soon the details were being worked out and Kathy noted all the information, including the number of guests who were coming, and the number who had not yet replied. Caroline and her aunt both knew from experience how people could still show up at the last minute.

And how some did not.

It was always best to be prepared, Caroline had learned. For the worst-case scenario.

Even when it came to cake.

"I believe we have an extra guest," Caroline said, adding a note beside her mother's name in her notebook, much as it pained her to see it in ink. "My mother told me that she's bringing a date."

Every eyebrow in the room shot up as the space fell quiet.

Finally, it was Aunt Sandra who said with a pout, "How on earth did Sharon find a date? She doesn't even hit the bars with me anymore!"

Caroline met Hillary's eyes and, despite herself, had to fight off a laugh.

She turned to Kathy, who looked equally confounded. "Is that what she's been up to these days, then? She's been secretive, busy on evenings when she's usually such a homebody. I can't believe she didn't tell me, though."

"I'm not the only one who didn't see this coming, then?" Caroline's sigh was heavy. "I still can't believe it. It feels official now that my parents aren't together. I know that my dad moved out in September, but I kept hoping it was just temporary. My parents were always so..."

"In love," Lucy said, tugging at her dark ponytail.

"Happy," Hillary commented, her shoulders slumping.

"Perfect," Kathy said simply.

Caroline blinked back tears and then recovered. "I didn't even think to ask the man's name. I was too shocked. I wonder if my father knows. He's invited to the wedding, but I don't see him listed as a confirmed guest."

"He hasn't RSVP'd," Sandra clarified. Gently, she added, "It was a courtesy invitation, dear."

Caroline let that sink in for a moment. And, meeting Kathy's eyes briefly, she wondered if hers had been, too.

But then she looked at Hillary, who seemed to be

frowning even deeper than she was, and she sensed that this wasn't the case at all. Hillary loved Caroline's father as if he were her own—maybe even in place of her own. It was Caroline's father who stepped in when Sandra's husband bailed on her, leaving her on her own with three little girls and bills she struggled to pay. It wasn't just a financial hand he'd lent at the time, but a supportive one, too. When Caroline learned to ride a two-wheeler, his hand had been right there on the back of Hillary's bike, too. Hillary and Mitch Baker might not be related by blood, but there was a bond between them that went back a lifetime.

"It won't feel right without Uncle Mitch there," she said quietly. She gave Caroline a watery smile.

Caroline's chest ached and she had to look away, not only because she couldn't imagine a family event where her father was noticeably absent, but because she knew that Hillary had probably said the very same thing recently—only about her.

"I am so sorry you had to see that," Kathy said when Caroline helped her carry the plates back into her industrial kitchen, which was considerably more organized than the one at Sweet Harmony. They were out of earshot now, and Caroline knew that she could speak frankly with her mother's younger sister.

She picked up a sugar cookie from a tray—still warm—and broke off a piece. It was sweet and soft in her mouth, and for a small moment she felt a little better. She could have eaten the entire thing had it not been for that darn maid-of-honor dress.

"I'm fine, really, Aunt Kathy." But even to her own ears, she didn't believe it.

"Are you sure?" Kathy looked at her earnestly with her dark eyes, and Caroline knew that she could tell her the truth. And that Kathy would patiently wait to hear it.

Caroline took another bite and chewed thoughtfully, taking a moment to savor the sweet taste of butter and sugar that made the simple cookie somehow dense and chewy and painfully addictive.

"I can understand getting roped into being the maid of honor. You and Hillary were so close growing up. But when I heard you were helping to plan the wedding..." Kathy pulled in a breath and shook her head.

"I'm honestly glad to be doing it," Caroline said, realizing as she said it that it was true. "It's given me something to focus on other than my own disappointment. And I love Hillary. You know how close we've always been. I do want her to have a beautiful wedding. And I want to support her, however I can."

"But?" Kathy stared at her frankly. She wasn't easily fooled. And she saw everything in this town.

Only unlike her aunt Marcy on her father's side, Kathy didn't repeat what she knew.

"But I do wish she wasn't marrying Tim," Caroline admitted.

For so many reasons.

"Don't we all?" Kathy said, making Caroline feel immediately more at ease. "After what he did to you?" She narrowed her eyes and clucked her tongue. "When I heard that little creep was sweet-talking our Hillary, well, I tried to intervene."

"You did?" Caroline didn't know this. But then, she didn't know a lot about what had been going on in this town in her absence. Her parents' separation, her mother's transformation, and her sister's reunion with Sean, to name a few.

"I suggested a few other guys to Hillary," Kathy said. "You know, sons of my regulars, guys in Boston who visit the Cape once or twice a year. I'd hate to lose Hillary to the city, but if it meant she'd be happy, then so be it."

Caroline considered her aunt's words—and her intentions.

She glanced over her shoulder into the storefront to make sure that they were still out of earshot. Hillary and Sandra were still looking through Kathy's portfolio while Lucy got the shop ready to open for the day.

"That's the thing, Kathy," Caroline said, dropping her voice to a whisper. "I'm not entirely convinced that Hillary is happy. But when I've pressed her, she's had a reasonable enough explanation to cover my doubts."

"The poor girl's probably a wreck worrying that Tim will do to her what he did to you," Kathy replied. "He's shown his true colors, and Hillary had a front-row seat."

"Maybe he's changed," Caroline said half-heartedly, and she almost laughed when she saw the no-nonsense look her aunt was giving her.

"For Hillary's sake, let's hope he has, my dear," Kathy said with a sigh.

Caroline gave her aunt a long hug when Lucy pushed through the door, announcing they had five minutes to get the display case filled, and rejoined her cousin and Sandra at the table, leaving her aunt and cousin in the kitchen to finish prepping before the weekend rush descended on them.

"So?" she asked. "Did I miss anything?"

"My mom was just telling me about *her* wedding cake," Hillary said.

Caroline stiffened. Sandra rarely talked about her husband, who had left her high and dry with three small children, rarely to be heard from again.

"It was a beautiful cake," Sandra said, smiling at the memory. "Homemade, of course, since I just had a backyard reception. Strawberry, and oh, I can still remember the taste of it. It seemed fitting for a summer wedding at the time, and it paired so nicely with the champagne. Of course, Donny wasn't thrilled about it being pink. He would have preferred chocolate, even for a wedding cake. I suppose I should have known then that he wasn't the man for me."

Hillary leaned forward. "Because of a cake?"

"The cake was just the first sign," Sandra said darkly.

Caroline and Hillary exchanged a look of alarm. They both knew that Sandra's marriage had not been a happy one. Her wedding had been a disappointment, and she wasn't shy in saying so, which was why seeing her daughters have a nice wedding day was all the more important to her.

And to Caroline.

"Well, this is going to be a beautiful cake," Caroline said firmly, forcing a bright tone and a smile. "Kathy makes the best ones around."

"It wasn't just the cake," Sandra said, still lost in the past. "We didn't agree on anything, as it turned out. Not where to live. Or how many children to have. Or how to raise them. But the wedding plans..." She narrowed her eyes. "That was the first sign. And if I'd paid more attention to that, I could have spared myself a lot of heartache and headache later on."

Hillary fell silent, and Caroline tensed up, glancing over her shoulder and wishing that her other aunt were here to diplomatically switch topics.

"But then I wouldn't have had you," Sandra suddenly rebounded. "Or your sisters. And for that, I would do it all over again. But..."

Oh, dear. Caroline darted her eyes desperately to the kitchen door, only to see Kathy bustling around through the window.

"It's better to avoid marrying the wrong man," Sandra said. "Better to avoid going down that bad path from the start. All the signs were there for me. I ignored them. I guess I thought if I did, everything would just eventually work out." She let out a bark of laughter that was so loud, both Hillary and Caroline jumped.

"Well!" With that, Sandra pushed back her chair and stood. "I better get back to the shop. I still have to finish all the dresses. *Especially* yours, Caroline. Stop by for another fitting in the next couple of days. And given the way the last fitting went, best to lay off the sweets," she whispered. Loudly.

"Sorry about that," Hillary said when Sandra pushed through the door, allowing a family with two small children to enter.

Which part? Caroline wanted to ask.

Instead, Caroline sat quietly with Hillary, letting her

aunt's words sink in, and even though only one of them was about to get married, and one of them had been jilted, Caroline was starting to wonder if she'd fared better than her cousin in the end.

Caroline eyed Hillary once they were alone on the sidewalk, sensing a shift in her cousin's mood. She hoped that the next stop on their list would cheer them both up a bit.

"If we hurry, we'll be the first people at the flower shop when it opens," she said.

But instead of looking pleased at the idea of sorting through buckets of flowers, which once would have been her cousin's idea of a perfect day, Hillary's forehead creased into a frown.

"Oh, I told Tim that I'd meet him for brunch today," she said. "I completely forgot! With all the stress for the wedding, it just slipped my mind!" She looked anxious as she pulled out her phone and checked the time. "I suppose that I could call him and tell him that it's not a good day..."

"Or I could handle the flowers on my own," Caroline offered.

"Flowers are so expensive," Hillary said, looking pained.

Caroline thought about what Lucas had told her, that as part of their deal, she couldn't reveal he was covering the costs. And why was that, exactly? Was he secretly harboring concerns that Tim wasn't as enthusiastic about this wedding as he should be?

"It's part of my profession to haggle," she assured Hillary.

"Okay, then I'll see you tonight?" Hillary looked questioningly at Caroline, who hesitated for a beat.

But of course. Molly had mentioned it last night over dinner. Tonight was Hillary's bachelorette party, the one part of this event that it seemed Caroline didn't have to worry about planning.

"I thought that was supposed to be a surprise," Caroline half-scolded.

Hillary shrugged, her smile finally lighting her eyes. "With a family as big as ours, someone's bound to slip. Besides, I prefer to know what I'm walking into."

That made two of them, only why hadn't Hillary started more actively planning her own wedding? Deciding not to stir up trouble where hopefully none existed, and telling herself that it was all on account of the short notice which would make anyone, even the most experienced event planner, feel overwhelmed, Caroline left her cousin to meet Tim while she walked down Main Street, knowing that even if she did manage to wiggle the price down a bit, the cost of the flowers was going to be steep. It was always one of the biggest items on the list of whichever type of event she planned—other than the alcohol bill.

And that brought her to another concern. Wine. Champagne. It didn't come cheap. Not for seventy people. The guest list was already cemented; there was no cutting back. And now, there was already one more addition, with her mother's date. Just thinking about it made her stomach hurt, and not just because it added to the bottom line.

She wondered if Lucas had any idea of just how much this wedding was going to cost him, and suspecting that he didn't and that she didn't want to cause trouble, she quickly sent him a text inviting him to meet her at the flower shop.

She was surprised when only a few seconds later, her phone pinged with a message telling her that he'd be there soon.

By soon, he meant immediately. Caroline stopped on the sidewalk when she saw him standing in front of the quaint storefront with the striped awning, looking more than a little out of place as he stood in front of the flower buckets perched on a stand outside, bending to smell some dahlias, which Caroline knew from experience didn't have much of a scent, however lovely they might be to look at.

She smothered a grin as she approached him.

"When you said you'd meet me here soon, you certainly weren't joking," she remarked by way of greeting.

He looked up from the flowers, giving her a funny look. "Most people wouldn't exactly call me the joking kind."

Caroline felt her cheeks flush. "I just mean... Well, you meant what you said about helping."

"I absolutely meant it," he said firmly. Then, peering at her, he said, "When will you have a little faith in me?"

That was a tall ask coming from the source, but she'd agreed to leave their past behind them, and besides, she enjoyed picking out flowers and didn't need to dampen the experience.

"I also happened to be grabbing coffee," he said, holding up a paper cup with her mother's café's logo stamped on the front of it.

Did he make a habit of frequenting Sweet Harmony often? That was nervy, all things considered. But then, she supposed that the Reynolds brothers were known for being shameless, weren't they?

"I'm just coming from the bakery," Caroline told him. "You'll be happy to know that the cake has been decided on, and my aunt is making it as a gift to the bride and groom."

"Did the appointment go well?" Lucas asked, and even though Caroline knew he was just making conversation, she hesitated, a part of her wanting to tell him that she wasn't so sure it had.

"Hillary said she's meeting Tim, which is why I'm here to look at the flowers," Caroline explained.

"Are you sure that's what she said?" Lucas frowned for a moment. "Because Tim's golfing with our biggest investor this morning and then rolling it into a working lunch."

"I must have misunderstood." Caroline's stomach stirred with unease. Maybe Hillary had made up an excuse, or maybe Tim had gotten his plans mixed up. Or maybe Tim was letting Hillary down. Either way, it was unsettling.

She had a looming headache by the time she pushed into the store, but her spirits were immediately lifted by all the colorful and fragrant blooms. She stopped to smell some peonies, breathing in their sweet scent, and then moved on to the roses, a classic that was sturdy enough to handle the strongest of ocean breezes.

Even though she and Hillary both agreed that white flowers would be best with the color scheme, she wanted to add some interest to the bouquets, and she walked over to the counter, craning her neck for the friendly gray-haired woman who had owned and operated the shop for as long as Caroline could remember.

"What about these?" Lucas asked from behind her, where he was pointing to a bucket of red roses.

Caroline wrinkled her nose. "The bridesmaid dresses are turquoise."

His dark eyes gleamed. "Oh, I know."

Caroline's body temperature rose and she struggled to look at him. "This is a beach wedding."

"So?" Lucas seemed so confused that Caroline had to struggle not to laugh. "I thought that women liked red roses."

Curious, she leaned a hip into the counter and stared at him. "Oh, so you have experience with this type of thing? Tell me, when was the last time you gave a woman flowers?"

He grinned with confidence. "Last month. For Mother's Day."

She felt a rueful tug at her mouth. So he was a good son, not that she'd ever had the opposite impression. Lucas was... dutiful. Maybe even...nice.

Before she could get too carried away with that thought, Sheila Fielding appeared from the back room, wiping water off her hands onto the sturdy green apron that bore the shop's logo.

"Why, Caroline Baker!" she exclaimed, her rosy cheeks lifting with her smile. "Isn't this a lovely surprise! What brings you back to town, and into my shop no less?"

"Wedding plans!" Caroline said brightly, unable to resist matching the shopkeeper's positive energy.

"Oh! Oh, honey! That is *wonderful*! Just *wonderful*!"

The shop owner's eyes went wide as she glanced over Caroline's shoulder. "Lucas Reynolds! And Caroline Baker! I had no idea! I must pop into Sweet Harmony at least three times a week and your mother never mentioned a thing. Neither did your aunt, come to think of it, and this type of news is fitting for her column..." Sheila looked at them both, puzzled.

"Oh." Caroline's cheeks were burning when Lucas came to stand beside her. He was so close that his arm brushed hers, and she inched to the side, nearly knocking a vase off a display table. "Oh, no. No. *I'm* not getting married."

Not again. Not...ever. By choice this time.

"And neither am I," Lucas said loudly and—Caroline couldn't help but notice—quite firmly.

She blinked a few times, startled by his proclamation, which seemed to extend beyond Sheila's innocent confusion, and then gave the older woman a watery smile. "I'm an event planner now, in Philadelphia. I'm in town helping my cousin with her wedding. Hillary's getting married."

"Of course." Sheila looked stricken. "I read all about *that* in the Harmony Happenings column." She pursed her lips.

Caroline sighed heavily. Aunt Marcy certainly knew how to spread the word.

Unfortunately, it hadn't reached Caroline in Philly. A heads-up would have been nice.

"But isn't that wedding soon?" Sheila continued, looking a little faint as the purpose of their visit became obvious.

Caroline hoped her expression didn't belay her own anxiety. It was entirely possible that Sheila wouldn't be able to accommodate them on such short notice, and she very much doubted that she'd have better luck in any shops in neighboring towns. It might come down to enlisting all the cousins to scour grocery store flower buckets after all, and if so, they'd make do. But for now, she'd try. For Hillary's sake, she had to.

As for Tim, he could take these flowers and—

"Next Saturday," Caroline confirmed with a nod. *One week from today*, she thought as her stomach rolled over not with excitement but with...dread. Nerves that were muddled with apprehension and unease that hadn't been there one week before her own wedding. But they should have been. "I understand it's very short notice."

"It is." Sheila sighed. "But I suppose it's better that way."

Caroline exchanged a glance with Lucas. Her heart pounded with hope. "Oh?"

"I'm closing my shop at the end of the month. If the wedding were any later, I'd have to decline altogether. As for pulling something together for next Saturday, I'm afraid my inventory will be quite limited given my circumstances."

Caroline couldn't bear the thought of anything more changing in Harmony Cove, not when she'd been away for so long, and not when she'd counted on it all being the same when—or rather if—she'd ever returned.

"Is someone else taking over?" she asked.

"I don't have any children who would want the shop. Michelle is a dentist," she said, beaming with pride. "And my Brianna just moved to the West Coast. My nephew in Boston is hardly an option. And it's not for everyone, running their own business, especially in a town so centered on tourism. Some days are better than others. Some years, too."

Caroline nodded. "I understand," she said, then lifted her chin when she saw Lucas turn to her sharply. "I mean, this type of business can be seasonal, too."

And entirely dependent on other people's spending habits and celebrations, or lack thereof. Oh, did she understand.

"It will be a shame to walk away from it, though," Caroline said, looking around the store, which had been tended with noticeable care.

"In the end, it's just a business," Sheila said with a shrug. "It's people who really matter."

Beside her, Caroline felt Lucas stiffen.

"I'll miss my clients, of course. But I'll see you around town still, won't I?" Sheila stared at her expectantly. "I could never leave the Cape. Or Harmony Cove. I mean, who could?"

Indeed. Who could?

"Oh…" Caroline had been so eager to leave when she'd first come back to Harmony Cove, but now, after easing into her new routine and being back with her family, she hadn't thought about Philly in days.

Because there was nothing waiting for her in Philly. Her phone hadn't pinged with a single new party request. And the only event she had to plan right now was here, in Harmony Cove.

"My business is back in back in Philly," she said to Sheila, who gave her a look of understanding but disappointment.

Only Caroline wasn't so sure that she did have a business still waiting for her back in Philly. And she couldn't stop thinking about what Sheila had said, too.

It wasn't the business that mattered. It was the people. And without her best friend running the event-planning company at her side, she wasn't sure that running it on her own would be enough to make her happy.

Or if it ever had been.

Eight

Lucas was aware that he was the last person who should be planning a party, yet here he was, putting beers on ice and unboxing pizzas, for the second time in three years.

The first time he threw his brother a bachelor party, he put a little more effort into it, going so far as to rent out a private room at a swanky bar in Provincetown. This time, he was keeping it a little more low-key, hoping that some good food, friends, and drinks would be enough to keep Tim's head in the game—and from straying too far from his immediate plans.

Or his bride.

The problem was that the Reynoldses didn't exactly have many friends in Harmony Cove. Lucas had always been content keeping to himself, and Tim, well, Tim had jilted one of the town's darlings, hadn't he? But Sean Morrison had moved back to town recently, and despite getting back together with Caroline's sister Annie, he didn't seem to hold any grudges, and the same went for Sean's cousin, Travis, whose reputation nearly exceeded Tim's when it came to women.

So there it was. The four of them, gathered in Tim's small but tasteful apartment that he'd soon share with Hillary, talking about sports, work, and, occasionally, the upcoming wedding.

"How long is your honeymoon?" Sean asked as he cracked open another beer.

Lucas sat a little straighter. He seemed to be the only person in the room who was anxious about Tim's response.

"Aren't most honeymoons a week?" Tim replied, reaching for a slice of pepperoni.

It wasn't exactly an answer to the question but Sean seemed satisfied enough by the response.

Lucas, however, was not.

"It's Saturday night," Travis said after helping himself to two slices of pepperoni and then polishing off a third. "What's the plan for the evening?"

Tim turned to Lucas expectantly as the room fell quiet. Across the living room, Lucas thought he saw Sean cover his grin with a napkin. He turned back to his brother, feeling guilty that he hadn't planned anything beyond this and annoyed that Tim was expecting more.

After everything.

Most people didn't get the red-carpet treatment twice in their life. But then, Lucas always rolled it out for his kid brother, and somewhere along the way, Tim got used to relying on him for it. Tim's needs were always met; Lucas had been sure of that.

But they weren't kids anymore.

And Tim... Tim hadn't shown any signs of growing up.

"There's the Bayview Bistro," Lucas suggested lightly, thinking that the outside deck with the view of the harbor might be nice on a night like this. And relaxed. Not too formal. Just the place for four guys to hang out, without all the wedding pressure he was hoping to avoid.

Tim shrugged and looked at their guests for approval. "What do you say?"

"I say," Travis said with a mischievous grin, "that so long as there are girls there, I'm in."

Lucas closed his eyes and stifled a sigh. This was exactly what he was hoping to avoid. Temptation. A glimpse at what Tim might be giving up by committing to one woman. Or too much joking about it, either. He'd been to bachelor parties back in Boston, mostly for coworkers who were now his employees. He knew how they went, and he knew that even though the jabs were in good fun, not everyone could take them.

And he worried that Tim couldn't. And he wasn't willing to take the chance.

"Girls?" Lucas frowned at Travis, whose reputation as the town flirt clearly hadn't changed in the years that Lucas had been away. But then, in a community like this, reputations tended to outlive most people. "Are you forgetting that this is a bachelor party? A chance for Tim to have a little guy time?"

"Before he spends the rest of his days chained to one woman?" Travis laughed loudly, and Lucas felt his jaw tighten. Sean glared at his cousin. Seeing that he didn't get the reaction he was looking for, Travis settled down and said,

"Whoa. I'm just joking, man. Besides, Tim may be getting married, but I'm still single. And last time I checked, so were you."

Yes, he was, and that was by choice.

Still, Lucas sighed and nodded. "The bistro it is," he said and hoped to heck that night wouldn't end in complete disaster.

Caroline sat on one of the armchairs in her cousin Lucy's small living room and sipped her champagne and smiled politely at all the stories her cousins were sharing, mostly about dates gone wrong, which seemed to subtly imply that Hillary was making the right choice by marrying Tim Reynolds, not the biggest mistake of her life.

She'd been in this very room a little over three years ago when the same group of girls had come together to celebrate her big day—even Annie had flown in from Seattle for the occasion. There had been champagne and cupcakes, compliments of the Bayview Bakery, only instead of having white frosting, the one on her plate today was a pale blue confection, and instead of the flowers on the coffee table and buffet being cream and blush roses, today's were a colorful mixed arrangement. But they did little to cheer her up.

"You haven't touched that cupcake," Molly said, coming to sit on the chair nearest her. "Are you doing all right?"

Caroline looked at her sister, wanting to open up and tell her that she wasn't sure how she felt, but then she caught a glimpse of Hillary across the room, laughing at one of their cousin Emily's stories, and she gave a wan smile.

"You remember how tight that dress was," she told Molly. "If I eat this cupcake, I might pop the seam on my walk up the aisle."

"That might make the front page of the *Herald*, knowing Marcy," Molly said with a laugh, and immediately Caroline felt a little better.

"What are we laughing about?" Val plopped down on the floor beside them both with the ease of someone all too used to getting down and playing with puppies.

"Aunt Marcy," Caroline said at the same time as Molly said, "Caroline's maid of honor dress."

Val's grin was wicked. "They are equally amusing for entirely different reasons. But if I were you, Caroline, I'd make sure that you get that dress situation under control before Marcy sees you in it. She'll lead her article with that."

"Is she even invited to the wedding?" Annie asked as she came to join the conversation, opting to seat herself on Caroline's armrest.

"Caroline should know," Molly said. "She's helping to plan it."

Annie didn't bother to hide her surprise. "You're what?"

Caroline stifled a sigh and glanced across the room to be sure Hillary couldn't hear them.

"I'm an event planner," she reminded Annie, who didn't seem mollified by the response. "I'm just helping out. Weddings are a lot of work, and I have the time and expertise."

Val and Annie exchanged a look but didn't argue the point.

"Hillary could use some more help if any of you are willing." Caroline thought of what she'd confirmed so far: the flowers would be ordered by tomorrow, once Hillary reviewed her options, and after leaving the shop, Caroline had put a call into a rental supply company for the ceremony seating and reception tent and tables. Putting food on said tables was another issue, and calls to nearby caterers had resulted in a series of rejections, along with a few shocked laughs at the timeframe.

Caroline supposed that if all else failed, they might rely on family connections and hold the reception on the patio of the Bayview Bistro, but she wasn't giving up just yet.

"Do any of you know a chef willing to cater on short notice?" she asked her sisters, who all shook their heads, as she knew they would. "What about a musician? We'll use a playlist for the reception but it would be nice to give Hillary some live music as she walks down the aisle."

And toward Tim Reynolds.

Caroline knew that her sisters were all thinking the same thing, but knew better than to say it.

"I know someone," Val offered. "One of my clients has a daughter who plays the violin. She's very good, and I know that she's always looking for professional opportunities. I'll be over there first thing tomorrow and I can talk to her then. If you come to my yoga class with me, I can tell you what she says."

Caroline preferred a good run to yoga, but she wasn't about to turn down an invitation from her sister. "That's settled then. And to answer your question, Marcy isn't invited to the wedding," Caroline said, having scanned and studied the guest list more than once.

"But when has that ever stopped her?" Val joked, relieving the tension that lingered.

While her sisters laughed, Caroline bit her lip. "Speaking of guests, I don't know if Mom mentioned anything to you guys…"

All three of her sisters stared at her blankly, giving her their full attention.

"Talk to us about what?" Annie asked.

Caroline hesitated and then sighed. "She's bringing a guest to the wedding. A…date."

The entire room seemed to go silent, and Caroline looked up to see that it wasn't her imagination. Every cousin had stopped their conversation and was now focused on the four Baker sisters and their never-ending family drama.

Hillary and Lucy already knew about this shocking development, of course, and gave her a look of sympathy.

"Your mom is dating someone?" Hillary's sister Phoebe said, looking as aghast as Caroline felt.

Molly stared at her with big eyes, bright with tears she was fighting back. "She hasn't said anything to me. But now that I think about it, she has been going out more. I can see from my window when she slips out in the evening, all dressed up, sometimes not getting home until after I've gone to bed. I assumed she was at all these new clubs she's joined."

"I'm beginning to think that these clubs were code for dates," Caroline said with a groan.

Val's lips were pursed. For once, she didn't have a quick comeback or remark.

"Do you think Dad has any idea?" Caroline asked Annie, knowing that the truth would come out eventually, especially in a town this small.

Especially with Marcy's ear to the ground. And every door and window, too.

Annie shook her head. "I don't think so," she said slowly. "But then, you know Dad. He wouldn't unload his problems on us. And he's private."

"Turns out that Mom is, too," Val grumbled, having found her voice. "I guess you can't really know anyone, can you?"

Caroline felt Hillary's stare from across the room and struggled to meet it.

No, she thought. You couldn't really know anyone. No matter how much you thought you did. They could let you down, disappoint you, and break your heart.

Only sometimes, she thought, as her mind drifted to Lucas, they could surprise you.

Any hope that Caroline held that the night might improve ended the moment their group took their party to the inn, where they were sure to get a discount at the Bayview Bistro.

"Sean!" Annie cried, perfectly delighted to spot her boyfriend.

Caroline immediately stiffened and glanced at Hillary,

who seemed equally surprised to see her fiancé and their small group of guys.

"We can go," Caroline offered quickly. "Really, we should go."

Meaning, *Please. Let's go.*

"It's your *bachelorette* party, Hillary," Molly concurred with wide eyes. "It's supposed to be a girls' night. Let's let the guys have this space."

But it was too late. Travis, being Travis, was waving to Hillary's sisters, who grinned back and walked over to greet him, quickly falling into conversation. Lucy looked at Emily, who shrugged.

"I can't stay long anyway," Emily said to all of them. "My mom is watching Juliet and I don't want to take advantage of her. You know how early she gets up."

"Oh, I do," Lucy said with a raise of her eyebrows. "Because I get up just as early to work with her at the bakery."

"I get up early, too," Molly chimed in, casting a guilty look at Caroline. They both knew the real reason that Molly wanted to leave was because she tended to shut down in unexpected social situations, especially ones including the opposite sex, and, of course, lingering conflict.

Caroline was just about to try to talk her sister into sticking around, but what she really wished was that she could find such a handy excuse. Unlike her cousins and sister, however, she didn't have to be at work at the crack of dawn.

At this rate, she wasn't sure when she'd even work again.

The mere thought of it was enough to make her stick around just to have a drink.

"Don't worry about staying on my behalf," Hillary assured them. Then, with a sigh in the direction of the guys' table, where Annie, Phoebe, and Kayla had already taken seats, she said, "It looks like the bachelorette portion of the night has ended anyway."

Caroline exchanged a glance with Val, who gave her a little frown.

So it wasn't just Caroline who thought it was odd that Hillary hadn't been a little more delighted about running into the man she was marrying in a week?

But then, it was supposed to be her bachelorette party. A girls' night.

One that, in hindsight, Caroline probably should have planned. If she had, she would have made darn sure that they didn't run into the Reynoldses.

But now they had, and after saying goodbye to Kathy's two girls and Molly, Hillary, Valerie, and Caroline moved over to join everyone else.

"Caroline Baker!" Travis Morrison's grin was wicked. "Long time no see! I heard you were back in town but I almost didn't believe it. Took a wedding to lure you back, did it?"

"I'm not—" Caroline felt Hillary watching her and stopped herself. "I'm not so sure it's been that long, Travis. You haven't changed at all since I've been away."

She wasn't just referring to his looks, which were good, and he knew it. From the way he was bantering with the twins, it was clear that he was still the town flirt, known to flit from woman to woman, and especially tourist to tourist.

But then, most people didn't change all that much, did they?

Her gaze drifted to Tim, who looked away when their eyes met. He cleared his throat and held out a hand to Hillary, then stood to give her his chair while he and Sean started grabbing a few more from neighboring tables.

Caroline made sure that she was at the far end of the table.

It seemed that Lucas had the same idea.

"Where's the rest of your group?" he asked once a round of drinks had been ordered.

"They went home," Caroline said with a heavy sigh.

Lucas leaned in and whispered, "You sound like you wish you could have joined them."

Caroline couldn't help it. She laughed. He'd called her out. Seen through her brave face. Straight to her true heart.

How was it that the one man who'd never seemed to look at her now saw her better than anyone else at this table?

"Bars aren't really my scene," she said, leaving it at that.

"Mine, either," he said with a wry grin.

In the darkness, his eyes looked almost black, and sitting this close, she could smell the musk of his skin mixed with the briny air. The heat of his body so close to hers was a sharp contrast to the cool evening breeze, and she felt a strange feeling in her stomach when he smiled at her like that —one that made her want to pull back.

And almost knock the drink out of Val's hand.

"Hey!" Her sister shot her a scolding look, but her

expression turned coy when she saw Lucas. "Oh, hello, Lucas."

"Hey, Valerie," he replied, a little stiffly, Caroline thought.

She frowned as she took a sip of her white wine. This was the side of Lucas that she'd always known, a little tense, awkward, and uncertain around people.

But the Lucas who had just made her laugh was different. And so was the person she'd been spending a lot of time with lately.

"You're shy," she suddenly said, once Val had joined a loud conversation at the other end of the table.

"Shy?" Lucas looked momentarily affronted and then relaxed his shoulders. "I wouldn't say shy, necessarily. I'd just say that big groups aren't my thing. And neither are social events. I'm not—" He stopped himself, looking away from her as he reached for his beer.

"You're not like Tim," she offered.

He glanced at her sidelong. "Someone in the family had to be responsible. Guess it's an oldest child thing."

He was downplaying a situation she'd witnessed firsthand. Tim was always the social one, always looking to have a good time, while Lucas was always worried about the fallout.

Given what had happened three years ago, Caroline realized that Lucas had a reason to always be so uptight around his brother. He'd seen past the charm and fun that Caroline enjoyed; he knew where it led.

"As the eldest in *my* family, I understand what it feels like to be responsible for your nest," Caroline said, thinking of her reasons for being here, and wishing that she could have found a way to intervene, to mend her broken family.

"I'm better one-on-one," Lucas said. "And I prefer to know what the topic of conversation will be."

In other words, he liked to feel in control. She got it. She wouldn't have her lists otherwise.

"Well, this is the first of the wedding events," she warned him with a grin. "So you'd better find a way to make it through all of them."

The look they exchanged was heavy, charged no doubt with the thought that it was possible the groom wouldn't make it all the way through.

Clearing her throat, Caroline said, "I'm a homebody, myself. No offense, but I'd way rather be in my bed with a good book and some fuzzy slippers right about now."

Now it was Lucas who laughed. "No offense taken. I'd like that, too. Minus the fuzzy slippers."

She grinned. The wine was going down easier. Maybe a little too easy. If it kept flowing as easy as this conversation, she might run the risk of actually enjoying herself tonight.

If she wasn't already.

"I would have thought you loved parties," Lucas said. "Given your profession."

"Well, don't let my clients know." Caroline lowered her voice and said, "I'm not always buying what I'm selling."

"That makes two of us," Lucas said wryly.

"What do you mean by that?" She was curious now, thinking of how he'd described the hotel.

The family experience.

The look on his face told her his answer, but he said,

"Let's just say that Tim's marriage would go a long way in reassuring some of our investors that the Reynolds family is the living, breathing image of the brand we're selling."

Caroline thought back to her clients, and what she revealed about herself. Would any of them want her planning their weddings or anniversary parties if they knew she didn't believe in lasting love?

Probably not.

"Your secret is safe with me." He lifted his beer to clink her glass. "You must enjoy it on some level, though, or you wouldn't do it."

Caroline thought about this. Planning a party and being a part of one were two very different things. Maybe over time, they'd simply become work. Or maybe she was just tired.

Or maybe she just hadn't found the right company.

Because right about now, she wasn't wishing she was at home in her slippers.

"I like making people happy," she said. "If I can be sure that someone's special event or celebration was a memorable moment or the day of their dreams, then I've given them more than a party."

He looked at her for a moment, his gaze roaming over her face until she shifted under his attention.

"Well, if I ever decide to host a party, you're the first person I'll call." Lucas opened his eyes wide. "I should have hired you to help me with the bachelor party, because something tells me that pizza and beer wasn't exactly celebratory enough, given that we ended up here instead."

Caroline grinned. "I'd say you did just fine. And unfortunately, bachelor parties aren't my area of expertise anyway."

"Just weddings, then?"

The question was casual, and Caroline realized with a start that he assumed that she did this all the time, plan a day for a happy couple, even when she didn't believe in happy endings.

She took a sip of her drink and set it down. "Actually, I don't plan weddings, either."

Lucas looked at her in surprise. "But—"

"It's not that I can't plan weddings," Caroline explained. "It's that I choose not to."

"Ah." Lucas nodded and took a long sip of his beer. After a moment, he shifted on his chair and looked at her.

Caroline squirmed under his dark gaze, wondering what he was thinking and not sure that she wanted to know.

Eventually, curiosity won out.

"You want to say more," she commented.

"Only to ask if you think you'll ever plan another wedding," Lucas said.

Her eyebrows shot up in surprise. "You mean after this one?" She had to laugh. It wasn't every day that a girl planned her ex-fiancé's nuptials. "That's a hard no."

He frowned. "No? Not for anyone?"

Caroline glanced at Annie, across the table, leaning into Sean, smiling up at his face, never looking happier.

She fought the pang in her chest, reminding herself that love was for the lucky. And even then, it didn't last.

Look at her.

Look at her parents.

"Oh, I think this is the last wedding I'll be planning," she said vaguely.

His brow furrowed. "But you're so good at it! And surely it won't be your last. There's always your own..."

But Caroline was quick to shake her head. "As for myself, I won't be planning a wedding because there will be no wedding."

"You don't plan to ever get married?" A strange look passed over Lucas's face as he looked at her. One that seemed a lot like sadness.

"It's a little hard to think of getting married when you don't believe in love," Caroline remarked, and then, realizing just how cynical she sounded, she grimaced. "Sorry. That must have sounded..."

"Refreshing. And I happen to share your sentiment. Everyone in town knows about my parents and their miserable marriage, and their even more miserable divorce." Lucas said the words lightly, but there was a shadow in his eyes. Rebounding, he pulled his drink closer and grinned. "My father didn't fare much better in Boston. Needless to say, I haven't exactly been inspired to try it for myself."

Caroline could only look into his sad eyes and share his pain, knowing that a comment wasn't necessary.

They both had pasts, and they'd both been burned. And they both stopped believing that love could last.

Even if it found them.

And much as Caroline thought that she'd never find a true connection again anyway, right now, she was starting to wonder if she'd been wrong.

About a lot of things.

Nine

When Valerie invited Caroline to join her for a class at Phoebe's yoga studio, Caroline could think of a dozen things she'd rather do than expose herself to that particular form of torture—including spending time with Lucas (not Tim) Reynolds, who wasn't turning out to be as bad as she remembered—unless that was the wine still talking. She had a looming headache from too little sleep and, admittedly, too many conflicting thoughts that only seemed to build by the day, but it was a Sunday morning, and her last in town, considering that she had booked a return flight to Philly for the day after the wedding.

And she was no closer to figuring out what was going on with her parents. Val, she knew, was her best bet at making progress.

"We're supposed to hold the position for a full ten seconds," Valerie said firmly when Caroline once again dropped to her mat.

Running was more her style. Even running in heels, like she did when she was handling an event. But balancing on one arm, bent over? No.

She felt her sister's eyes on hers, even though Val's head was currently upside down with her long dark ponytail skimming her mat, and tossed up her hands. "I'm here for you, not the class," she whispered, even as she welcomed the chance to be kicked out of the studio for lack of participation.

"Then you should have told me as much and we could have skipped this and gone straight for the smoothies," Val hissed, earning a narrowed glance from Phoebe, who clearly wasn't giving them any preferential treatment for being related.

Sorry, Caroline mouthed to her cousin, who just pursed her lips to hide her smile and then slid into another pose that Caroline had no hope of attempting without risk of injury or humiliation—and she'd had her share of that in this town.

"That was hard work," Caroline said once she and her sister were finally seated at a sidewalk table at Common Grounds, blended juices in hand and the sun on their faces.

"Not if you keep at it," Valerie said. "Move back to town and Phoebe and I will have you holding poses for thirty seconds within a week."

"Thanks, but I think I'll stick with Philadelphia." Caroline took a sip of her strawberry smoothie, but it didn't go down easily this time.

Across the table, Val looked disappointed. "Darn. I was sort of hoping that now that you've been back, you'd want to stay."

Caroline couldn't admit that the thought had crossed her mind, not when staying in Harmony Cove seemed almost as impossible as leaving it again. She didn't have an apartment anymore. Sure, her mother would take her in, but if her mom's love life was getting as serious as they all feared, then three would soon be a crowd.

And of course, she didn't have a job here.

Even if she wasn't sure she still had a business back in Philadelphia.

And then of course there was the small fact that Tim Reynolds had moved back to the Cape.

"You must be thinking of our other sister," Caroline deflected. "I have to say that I'm still surprised that Annie moved back."

"Are you, though?" Val tipped her head thoughtfully. When she scrunched up her nose, the dusting of freckles on her skin was obvious. "She didn't really love her job in Seattle, as it turned out. Sean had returned, and she was willing to take a chance on him. And Dad retired, so now she can run the paper, which, of course, she was always destined to do."

It was true. Ever since they were little girls, Annie had taken an interest in the family newspaper, tagging along with their father to the office on weekends or summer mornings, and trying to re-create a weekly tabloid at home based on the happenings under the Baker roof.

The younger Annie could have had a field day with the events that had transpired in the last few years.

"Speaking of Dad," Caroline said, getting back to the matter at hand. "I wonder if one of us should warn him about Mom having... Well, I don't want to say the word *boyfriend*, but is that what it is?"

Val grimaced. "Does that term work at her age?"

Caroline laughed. "Mom and Dad are not that old."

Val just shrugged. "Can we call him her beau?"

Now it was Caroline who winced. "Can we just pretend he doesn't exist?"

"I don't see how that's possible when we'll be face-to-face with him Saturday night. Or Friday, if he comes to the rehearsal dinner, too."

"I hadn't even considered this," Caroline said, sinking her forehead into her hand. Friday's event was being held at the café, and there was no reason why their mother wouldn't invite her *beau* to a party she was hosting. "I haven't had much part in the planning of the rehearsal dinner. I trusted Mom to handle it."

"At least we'll all be there for support," Val assured her, leaning across the table to pat her hand. Before Caroline could say anything more, her mouth twitched. "And so will Lucas."

"Lucas?" Caroline snatched her hand back. "What are you talking about?"

"Just that you seem to enjoy his company. He makes you laugh." Her eyebrows shot up to underscore how surprising she found this.

Caroline didn't mention that this made two of them.

"Talking to him was better than facing Tim or putting up with Travis," Caroline pointed out.

"I'm just saying that you seem to get along," Val remarked, her tone pitched with insinuation.

"Please," Caroline scoffed. "You know exactly how I feel about Lucas."

Only that wasn't true anymore, was it? Her feelings had shifted, growing from contempt to just...vague disdain. Borderline tolerance at best.

Occasional glimmers of enjoyment, sure.

Certainly nothing more than that.

"I was walking Pepper yesterday morning and saw the two of you outside the flower shop. You seemed more than content in his company," Val suggested. "Twice in one day, too!"

"He's giving some input on the wedding plans," Caroline informed her sister. "It's easier than dealing with Tim."

Val sat straighter and gave her a look of sympathy. "Of course. I wasn't trying to be insensitive."

"You weren't," Caroline assured her. "And Lucas isn't so bad, I guess."

Not as bad as he used to be, at least, which she supposed was a low bar indeed.

"And he's not the only person helping with the wedding plans," Caroline reminded Val. She felt a prickle of nerves even though this wasn't her wedding. "Were you able to talk to your friend about the music for the ceremony?"

"She's thrilled to do it. Even offered her services free of charge. She said she's never played at a wedding before so it will give her some street cred."

Caroline shouldn't be surprised that Val had come through. Still, knowing that she had was another reminder of the loyalty of family that certainly couldn't be found outside of this town.

Her phone rang, putting a merciful end to this ridiculous conversation. She reached into her tote bag to fish it out, then frowned when she saw the name on the screen, and her relief was replaced with panic when she saw her sister's expression.

"Well, look at that," Val remarked, her eyes dancing. "Lucas has your number? And you have his stored in your phone? My, my."

"Stop," Caroline said, but she couldn't fight the flutter in her stomach when she connected the call. He *had* made her laugh last night, on an evening that could have been pretty miserable otherwise. "Lucas?"

"I hope I didn't catch you at a bad time," he said. Ever polite. Ever so rigid.

It might have bothered her in the past. Now, she didn't mind it so much. Maybe because she understood it a little better.

"I just finished a yoga class, so I'm free," she said, then gritted her teeth. "Not free. I mean...now's a good time to talk."

Wow, she really was out of practice when it came to talking to men. And she definitely wasn't used to talking to them on the phone, outside of business, that was.

But wasn't that what this was, really?

"I was calling to see if you have dinner plans," Lucas surprised her by saying.

Caroline swallowed hard as her eyes darted to her sister, who was slurping her banana smoothie, watching her shamelessly. A couple with a black Labrador rounded the corner and Val's expression transformed as she greeted what was clearly one of her clients, scratching the Lab behind the ears until the dog happily licked her face.

"Dinner?" Caroline repeated in a whisper as her heart started to pound.

Sure enough, Val's head jerked toward her, her canine friend all but forgotten as it trotted away with its owners.

"Tomorrow night. There's a restaurant in Chatham. I've been considering the chef for the hotel's signature restaurant, and needless to say he's willing to do us a favor by catering the wedding in exchange for a fair shot at the job."

"Is that…ethical?" Caroline asked but then rolled her eyes. Since when did the Reynolds men care about ethics? They did what suited them, always.

"Let's call it business," Lucas replied with a chuckle that made her soften her stance.

But only a little.

"I could use your input on the menu," Lucas explained. "For the wedding."

"Of course," Caroline said. For the wedding. It was a matter of business. For the wedding.

It was absolutely nothing more than that. The fact that it was a dinner on a Monday night was proof of it. There was absolutely no reason for her to be getting worked up or nervous about the thought of sharing a meal with this man. She'd had dozens of tastings over the years with clients. Lucas was nothing more than that.

"So…" Val said dramatically once Caroline had disconnected the call. "Did I hear something about dinner plans with Lucas Reynolds?"

"For the wedding," Caroline told her sister firmly.

Because that's all that was going on. Nothing more than that. Nothing at all.

"In that case, we'd better go shopping," Val said. "Something tells me that you're in need of a dress."

Caroline wished that she could say that this wasn't the case, but as usual, Val had a way of being right.

About everything.

Besides, she did have to stop by Sandra's shop for a second fitting...

And from the triumphant look on her sister's face, she knew it.

It wasn't uncommon for Lucas to go into the office on Sundays. He viewed the day like any other, and he preferred the quiet that the weekend brought, without the construction noise or activity on the jobsite. It allowed him to get ahead for the week and feel like he had a better handle on the upcoming projects, but today, he felt out of sorts and restless.

The wedding was less than a week away. Hopefully, by this time next week, Tim and Hillary would be on their way to their honeymoon, wherever that would be, and Wallace would be patting Lucas's back, talking about what a great party it had been.

He'd feel better once he'd cleared this hurdle, once he was back on good terms with his biggest backer. When he felt sure that one wouldn't pull out, leaving him to halt construction of the project.

He was surprised when, halfway through the afternoon and his third cup of coffee, Tim opened the door of the trailer.

"You forget something?" Lucas remarked, setting down the sandwich he'd picked up at Sweet Harmony. He'd stopped in because it was the best casual spot in town, or so he'd told himself. Just like he'd told himself that his disappointment over not seeing Caroline there was only because she could assure him that this wedding wasn't just going to be beautiful, but that it would be successful.

For Tim. For the family. For the business.

"Ha." Tim didn't look amused. "Believe it or not, I do work."

Lucas stayed silent, opting to take a bite of his food. Working was one thing. Working hard was another.

As if reading his mind, Tim pivoted from the coffee stand where he was making a cup. "Not everyone marries their work like you do, Lucas."

"You know I'm not the marrying kind," Lucas replied, wishing he'd stayed silent the moment the words slipped out.

It was just the kind of opening his brother needed to admit that he wasn't, either. But Tim said nothing, instead focusing on adding cream and sugar to his coffee, the way he liked it.

"So," Lucas said, setting aside the sandwich. "We didn't get a chance to talk much at the party. How did it go with Steve yesterday?"

Tim took a sip of his drink and then shrugged. "Oh, you know Steve."

Yes, Lucas did know Steve, and as much as he liked to

have a good time, when it came to money, it was no joking matter. And as their second biggest investor, he had a lot at stake with this project.

But he also knew that Tim's charm was enough to reassure him that his investment was sound. It didn't matter that Lucas had made sure that ground broke on schedule, or that he had all the permits in place well in advance, clearing the path for a smooth project. It didn't matter that he'd held up his end of the bargain, or that when he gave his word, he meant it.

Steve liked working with Tim. Even if that work mostly ended on the ninth hole.

Lucas supposed he should be relieved rather than annoyed. It freed him up to worry only about Wallace, who seemed determined to find faults, even where none existed. Maybe he was just impatient. Maybe he was skeptical.

But Lucas was, too. And right now, he had a bad suspicion that Wallace was just looking for an excuse to pull out of this project. Lucas already had his lawyers reviewing the contract, preparing for any loophole Wallace would find to back out.

And right now, Lucas's biggest worry was the morality cause.

This was a family resort. And the Reynoldses would have to uphold a reputation worthy of that pitch.

"I take it you let Steve win?" Lucas pressed, meaning that Tim had better have let the guy win. Steve had a terrible putt and Tim was one of the most competitive guys around, but even Tim knew when to put his ego aside for a few hours.

"Yes, I let him win." Tim sighed heavily. Then, with a flash of a wicked grin, he said, "By one stroke."

"Tim!" Lucas bellowed. But he fought off a belly laugh that rose up in him, the anger outweighing it. This was the thing about Tim. He was so predictable it was infuriating. And that was what made Lucas so tense right now. He knew his brother. He knew him better than anyone. Better than Caroline ever knew him. Definitely better than Hillary.

He'd known that Tim wasn't going to go through with marrying Caroline. Deep down, he was ashamed to admit that he'd hoped he wouldn't. He just hadn't expected him to wait until the last minute to call it quits.

And right now, all signs were pointing toward him not going through with this wedding, either.

Unless Lucas made sure that he did.

"Did you invite him to the wedding?" Lucas asked, meaning, *Will there still be a wedding?*

Tim didn't seem fazed as he began riffling through a stack of mail from Friday.

"I gave him an invitation. Has he RSVP'd yet?"

"I wouldn't know," Lucas replied.

"Wouldn't you, though?" Tim raised an eyebrow. "Seems like you and Caroline have been helping out with some of the plans."

In a town this small, Lucas supposed that some chatter was bound to happen. Caroline had promised him that she wouldn't mention that he was paying for this wedding, and he trusted her.

Unlike his brother, she kept her promises.

"Caroline's an event planner. She's helping Hillary, and I'm helping Caroline. On your behalf." Both he and Tim would benefit from this wedding being one that people—especially Wallace—would remember for the right reasons. The price tag was an investment in both their futures—for Tim both professionally and personally. "Unless you wanted to brainstorm with your ex?"

"I figured that Hillary had it all under control," Tim said with a shrug. He gave Lucas a long look, as if he had more to say, but then changed his mind. He walked over to his desk. Standing on the other side of the partition, he was still visible.

"Did you see Hillary yesterday before the party, then?" Lucas asked lightly, thinking back on what Caroline had said about the couple meeting for brunch—when Tim was supposed to be wining and dining Steve.

"No, Hillary was busy with her mother yesterday," Tim replied. "Some appointments for the wedding. You know I don't pay much attention to that kind of stuff."

No, he didn't, and that was just the problem.

"So you didn't...have brunch?"

Tim frowned at Lucas. "Did you forget the conversation we just had? I was golfing with Steve all morning followed by lunch. Burgers and Bloody Marys."

Yep, that sounded like Tim's version of a business meeting.

So Hillary hadn't gone to meet Tim for brunch. Meaning that either she'd been lying to Caroline. Or Tim had canceled on her.

Either way, Lucas didn't like it.

But he had a very bad feeling that there was very little he could do to stop whatever was happening between the two of them. Even though he'd try. Just like last time, he'd try.

Because this time, he had more to lose.

Ten

Caroline and Lucas had agreed to meet at the restaurant in Chatham rather than drive together—which Caroline suspected they both silently agreed would make this feel a little too personal. It was just a dinner meeting, she told herself all day, and later, when she was zipping up the dress that she'd bought at Sandra's shop, still wondering what had been worse: the second gown fitting or Val's way of playfully pushing dresses with shorter and shorter hemlines (and lower and lower necklines) at her.

Now, as she turned down the crushed seashell drive that led to the waterfront restaurant, Caroline wished that she'd brought one of her business suits with her from Philly—not that it had seemed needed at the time. But it would have sent a clear message, one that wouldn't blur the lines, because this restaurant, with its gray shingles and strings of bulb lights hanging over the porch that was edged with overflowing flowerpots, screamed one thing and one thing only: romance.

Nervously, she pulled to a stop next to what she assumed was Lucas's car: a large black SUV with tinted windows. It was only as she stepped out and adjusted the skirt of her dress that she realized that there were no other cars in the lot.

She was just about to cross-reference the name of the restaurant he'd texted her with the one on the sign in front of her when the door to the unassuming car beside her opened, and Lucas stepped out.

Caroline jumped, then set a hand to her racing heart. "You scared me!"

"You knew I was meeting you here," he replied casually, his mouth twitching.

"Yes, but I assumed inside... I didn't see anyone in the car." She stopped, taking a moment to catch her breath and look around the empty lot. It was an easy excuse not to look his way, or notice that he was more dressed up than he had been at their last social gathering, too, in khaki pants, a white linen button-down shirt, and a navy blazer. A tie might have felt more professional. His jaw was clean-shaven, his skin smooth and slightly sun-kissed, and his dark eyes never strayed from hers, until she looked away, motioning to the empty gravel lot. "There's no one here. Are you sure they're open?"

"They're not," Lucas said, grabbing her attention once more. "The restaurant is closed on Mondays. We're here for the tasting menu.

"Shall we?" Lucas asked, extending an arm by invitation.

Caroline nodded and then joined him as they walked toward the main entrance, pausing only to let him open the door for her. Inside, the restaurant was dimly lit by a single lamp on each table and a fireplace that anchored the dining room, which she assumed was permanently lit for ambiance. The design was a mixture of rustic and elegant finishes, with a wall of paned windows at the back that overlooked a stunning terrace with a wide view of the sea.

"This is a beautiful restaurant," she commented.

"The one at the hotel will hopefully be even better," Lucas said. He stood a little straighter when a portly man in chef's whites came into the waiting area with his hand extended. "Chef Isaac." Lucas shook the man's hand aggressively and made the introductions. "Thank you for agreeing to accommodate us tonight."

"The thanks is all mine," the chef replied. "My team and I have put together a very special menu for you tonight. Would you prefer to sit in the dining room or on the terrace?"

"Terrace," Caroline said at the same time as Lucas. They shared a small smile. As lovely as the interior was, it was too nice of a night to stay indoors, and she longed to enjoy the ocean air for as long as she still could.

"Terrace it is," the chef said, quickly leading them through the main room and out onto the patio. A salty breeze blew at Caroline's hair and filled the air, making her wish for a moment that she'd worn it up—but she hadn't, if only because Val had urged her to. They were seated at a table with an unblemished view of the water and immediately presented with glasses of champagne.

The chef reviewed the menu for them, all of which sounded delicious, and then promptly left them to return to the kitchen.

Alone like this, Caroline suddenly felt conspicuous. She took a small sip of her drink, not just because she was driving, but because she needed to keep a clear head tonight.

It would be too easy to get swept away in a place such as this one. But a professional dinner was all that this was.

For some reason, though, this one felt different. Maybe it was because she was back in Harmony Cove. Or maybe it was because she was with Lucas. And he was turning out to be much different than she'd once thought.

Finally, when she couldn't stand the tension any longer, she said, "If the food is half as good as the ambiance and service then I think this is your chef."

Lucas darted a glance over his shoulder to make sure they were not being overheard. "I hope so. If things go well tonight, I intend to make him an offer."

"What makes you think he'll be the best choice for the hotel? Other than the obvious." She swept her arm over the tastefully decorated terrace.

Lucas paused to consider his answer. "It's his warmth that I'm after. His roots in the Cape. His insistence on keeping things local. He's young, but he's an old soul."

Caroline smiled at him until he cocked his head.

"What?" he finally asked.

"Nothing," she said lightly. Then, sensing that he wanted a real answer, she said, "It's just that you're sentimental about Harmony Cove. It's about more than all the details for you. You want the hotel to embody everything you feel about the place."

He nodded. "Harmony Cove is special. I realized it even more when I was living in Boston. Every time I visited, I never wanted to leave again. Maybe it takes distance to make you really appreciate what you have. When I was growing up, this was just home, but now... Well, I'm proud that it is. I may keep to myself, but at the end of the day, I know that there's a community, and there's something comfortable in that. Especially when..."

"When you didn't exactly have the support you needed at home?" she ventured, keeping her tone deliberately gentle.

He nodded. "My mother rebounded from the divorce from my father. And from her husband after that. She's realized she's happier on her own. She has everything she needs on the Cape. And I do, too."

Except for a wife. Or children.

Caroline decided not to press that point.

"If you're so sure that this chef is the perfect fit, why not offer him the job instead of going through all this?"

But it was about the wedding, of course. It was thanks to Lucas that they might not end up at the bistro after the wedding ceremony.

"Sometimes people want something more when they feel they've earned it," Lucas said. He looked out onto the water for a moment. "My father didn't just hand over the company —not to me, at least. I had to prove myself over the years to earn the title."

"And Tim?" Caroline already knew the answer, because she'd witnessed it firsthand. Tim was happy to coast and settled in the comfortable position of being the boss's son.

Lucas met her eyes. "Tim always knew my father would keep him on board, and Tim didn't care about leading the charge. Don't get me wrong, I love what I do, but I also know how hard I had to work to get to where I am today. Sometimes it's the struggle that leads to gratitude. And...perspective."

Caroline was surprised to hear Lucas say anything less than positive about Tim, but she didn't exactly feel like feeding into it. Instead, she considered her own setbacks.

"Every time I get a new client for my business, I feel like it's the first one all over again." She smiled, thinking of how exciting that first client had been. How she and Maya had popped champagne and toasted to a long future together. How she'd felt so proud of herself for finding success after a failed engagement.

Little did she know then that all too soon, her plans would once again come to a grinding halt.

"You like what you do." Lucas made this a comment, not a question.

Caroline supposed it was obvious, or she wouldn't be planning her cousin's wedding to her ex. "I love it. But...it's not the easiest business. I'm dependent on other people's word of mouth, and not everyone has the budget for a big party. Some people opt to plan it themselves. Others don't have anything to celebrate. Then there are those who are forever a guest, never a host. Some people have small families or circles of friends and don't need my help."

Lucas nodded. For a moment, Caroline worried that he would bring up Tim again, but instead, he turned it back to business. "I like a good challenge, too. Between us, the business took a big hit with the lack of interest in large office spaces, and I've been doing some damage control ever since taking things over. Building this hotel is the next step to getting things back on track and starting a new future. A better one, hopefully."

"So you think you're here to stay, then?" Caroline was surprised, if only because Lucas's personality didn't exactly fit in with the laidback lifestyle. She couldn't remember ever seeing him in swim trunks, and she nearly laughed out loud at the mere idea of him splashing around in the water like they all used to do as kids. Lucas seemed to forever be an adult, even as a child.

But then, she was starting to wonder just how much she knew about Lucas Reynolds. And how much she had only assumed.

"The Cape isn't just a beautiful place. It's my home," he replied with a firm nod. "And if I can make this project a success here, on my own turf, then I will have everything I need in life. And I do intend to make it a success."

"Of course," she said, having no doubt that he would do just that. Unlike his brother, Lucas was someone who saw things through. Who fought for what he wanted. Tonight was an example of that. "It's just that most people want it all, as you might say. You only want the business?"

She felt a heat flare up in her cheeks, and she wished she hadn't pushed the topic, afraid of how it might come across, but Lucas didn't seem fazed.

"Maybe a dog. If I can make the time to give it the life it truly deserves."

She stared at him, not sure whether to laugh or cry, wondering how one brother could be so vastly different from the other, and in ways that she hadn't noticed or appreciated before. She didn't have long to consider it when the chef reappeared with their first course: a large grilled scallop on a bed of microgreens, paired with white wine.

Caroline and Lucas wasted no time tucking in. The fish was sweet and buttery, and they didn't speak again until they'd cleared their plates.

"I think I was hungry." Caroline laughed and took a sip of the crisp wine.

"I think I'll be making this guy an offer. And saying a prayer that he accepts." Lucas blew out a breath.

It was the first time that Caroline had seen Lucas be anything but confident.

"He must want the job or he wouldn't be willing to cater a wedding...this Saturday." She frowned at how quickly the day was approaching, even though, after tonight, most of the plans would be settled. The chairs and tables had been rented. The flowers were ordered. Music was locked in, thanks to Val. Even her maid of honor dress seemed to fit a little better. "After this, I think we're set."

"While we're on the subject of plans, did a man by the name of Steve happen to say if he's coming?"

Caroline thought back to some of her texts with Hillary. "Yes. Another last-minute guest, not that I don't factor such things in. Why?"

Lucas bristled. "He's just someone I know, is all."

Caroline peered at him. "Another very important person?"

"Another investor," Lucas replied. "It's not uncommon to invite business acquaintances to weddings."

No, it wasn't, but Caroline sensed that there was more to these particular invitations.

The chef appeared again, this time with the main course: lobster tail with risotto.

"If this is as delicious as the first course, then it will officially be the best thing I ever ate," Caroline gushed, then glanced at Lucas, hoping she hadn't gone too far.

But he was smiling at her. Smiling in a way that made her stomach go a little funny and her cheeks flame.

"And if there is anything you'd like to suggest before your wedding day, I would be more than happy to tweak the recipe or include something that is meaningful, just for the two of you," the chef said warmly, taking a slight bow.

Caroline felt the silence wash over the terrace, only the call of the seagulls interrupting her thoughts. She gaped at the chef, afraid to even so much as glance at Lucas, who finally cleared his throat.

"The wedding is actually for my brother," she heard Lucas say.

For some reason, and maybe more than one, she felt her spirits sink a little on that statement. Tim was getting married. Again. Or for the first time, really. And Lucas had no intentions of ever marrying anyone. And certainly not her.

And why that bothered her, when she herself had sworn off love, she really couldn't say. It was the atmosphere, she supposed. The pink-streaked sky. The strings of lights that glowed in the sunset. The sound of the ocean waves in the near distance lulling her into a feeling of false calm.

"My apologies," the chef said, looking genuinely mortified. "I just assumed...a handsome couple such as yourself..."

"We're not a couple," Caroline said this time. She gave

the poor man a reassuring smile. "Just...two people with the same goals."

"We have the same goals, do we?" Lucas asked once they were alone again.

Caroline took a bite of her food, savoring the taste of the fragrant herbs. It was true, in many ways they did. They both loved the Cape, even if only one of them lived here. They both took commitment seriously, which she would be the first to admit surprised her.

And they both had no interest in getting married, which saddened her more than she'd ever dared to really think about before tonight. All this time, she'd told herself that she was guarding her heart by keeping to herself, that she was better off alone than with the wrong man. But now, the thought of never having a family of her own, when her own was falling apart and coming undone, filled her with a sense of loss.

She gave a firm nod, reminding herself of why she'd come to dinner tonight. "We both want this wedding to be more successful than mine."

As soon as she'd said it, she wished she could take back the words. The expression on Lucas's face confirmed that he felt the same.

"Besides, what was I supposed to say to the guy?" she said quickly. "We're just two people that have known each other for years but somehow have never really known each other, coming together to make sure that my ex-fiancé has a great wedding reception...to my cousin?"

She'd meant to lighten the mood, but Lucas didn't

laugh. Instead, he set down his fork. "You don't think we ever knew each other?"

Caroline stared at him, trying to hide her shock while figuring out how to reply to such a preposterous statement.

Honesty, she decided. If there was one thing she'd learned from the Reynolds men, however indirectly, it was that honesty was always best.

"I was in and out of your house for years and we barely exchanged ten words with each other," she pointed out. "The most you have ever said to me, other than this past week, was when you came to the church and told me that Tim was a no-show, and even then, you kept things brief. It doesn't keep me up at night, Lucas, but it was clear you weren't my biggest fan."

"Is that really how you see me?" Lucas's pinch between his brows deepened.

Caroline set down her wine glass. "Are you telling me that you have a different recollection?"

Lucas tipped his head from one side to the other and then shook it softly. "Not exactly."

"It's okay." Caroline resumed eating. She was not going to let such a delicious meal go to waste, and she certainly wasn't going to let another day of her life be soured by a Reynolds brother. They'd done enough damage. "Some people just don't click. So you never liked me. No hurt feelings."

At least, not entirely. It was impossible not to feel stung when she remembered his cold and callous delivery on her wedding day. The way his eyes looked like two dark stones.

The way he stared at her as her world fell apart, and then walked away as quickly as possible.

"Why would you think I didn't like you?" Lucas said, breaking the silence.

She stared at him over her wine glass. "Lucas. Come on. I just told you."

"I know." He wiped his mouth and set the napkin back in his lap, looking at her intensely. "I know what you said, and I know where you're coming from. But you couldn't be more wrong. About...all of it."

She stared at him, not sure what to believe. "Every time you were around Tim and me, you would stare at me with this...this judgmental look on your face."

Now it was Lucas who laughed, throwing Caroline off-balance. She hadn't insulted him then, not that she intended to.

"Maybe I did," Lucas said, still looking amused as he sipped his wine. "But not for the reasons you think."

She stared at him, trying to make sense of where he was going with this, unsure if she even wanted to know. The past was in the past and she preferred to leave it there. Besides, did it even matter now? Tim was marrying Hillary. At least, for Hillary's sake, she hoped he was.

She'd accepted it. She'd...moved on. She hadn't thought it possible but somehow, this week, she really had. Maybe it was coming back to Harmony Cove. Maybe it was seeing Tim again, and realizing that there was nothing left between them. No pitter-patter of her heart. No flutter of her stomach.

Or maybe...it was something else. Or someone else.

Lucas leaned forward on the table until she had no choice but to stare into his deep-set eyes and wait for whatever it was he was about to say.

"You want to know the reason I was always staring at you and Tim like that?"

Caroline's heart started hammering in her chest, so loudly that she was sure he could hear it over the roar of the ocean waves and the call of the birds. Was there no music in this place? Without other diners, there was no avoiding Lucas, not unless she stood up and walked away.

But that was a coward's game. That was Tim's way.

Besides, what did she think Lucas was going to say? What was the worst he could say?

"I know you never approved of me marrying Tim," she finally said.

One eyebrow rose. His stare never wavered.

"You're right. I didn't."

Just like that, all the good feelings were knocked out of her as forcefully as the tide, bringing her back to her senses. Leave it to Lucas Reynolds to just put it out there, however bluntly.

"And the reason I didn't approve, the reason I might have seemed...judgmental...was because I always wondered what the heck a smart, pretty, loyal, and kindhearted girl like you was doing with a guy like Tim."

Caroline felt her eyes widen in surprise, and for the second time in a matter of seconds, her breath stopped.

They stared at each other for a long, telling moment, until the chef came outside once more, this time delivering the most decadent chocolate dessert she'd ever seen in her life.

"Of course, at the wedding there will be cake, but I couldn't let you leave tonight without trying our signature mousse," he said with a flourish.

There was one dessert. Two spoons. And this was technically a business dinner.

But it didn't feel like a business dinner anymore. And for some reason, she was fine with that.

She picked up a spoon and slipped Lucas a small smile across the table.

"Shall we?"

"I never could resist chocolate," he said, grinning like a little boy.

She hid her smile by taking a bite. Neither could she.

Just one more thing in common.

Not that she'd be admitting it.

Eleven

Like so many mornings growing up in Harmony Cove, the Baker sisters started their day at their mother's café. Molly joined them after finishing her prep work in the kitchen, and set a platter of assorted pastries on the table in the middle of their cups of coffee.

Caroline wasted no time reaching for the blueberry scone, her personal favorite. She broke off a piece and let it melt in her mouth, savoring the buttery sweetness.

"Did you make these or Mom?" she asked her youngest sister.

"I did," Molly said proudly.

Even though they'd all taken turns helping their mother in the kitchen at both their home and the café since they were children, only Molly had shown a real interest in the culinary arts, but even she could never compete with their mother's cooking or baking. Their mother had a special way of knowing how to add just the right amount of salt or sugar to a recipe.

But it would seem that Molly had come a long way since Caroline had been gone.

"My little sister is growing up," Caroline said with a sigh, giving her a dramatic wink.

"I'm not so little." Molly bristled. "You've been gone for three years, after all."

As if Caroline wasn't aware of exactly how long she'd kept away from this town—or why. Tim might have been gone for most of that time, but the memories of that awful day still lingered here—or so she'd feared. Now, sitting at a corner table at Sweet Harmony, surrounded by her sisters, with faces she recognized from childhood filling out the remaining space, she wished that she had faced her fears sooner.

It might have been less lonely than hiding from them.

"Enough talk about scones," Valerie said with an impatient sigh. She looked around the table at their sisters and announced, "Caroline had a date last night."

Annie audibly gasped, and Molly had to stifle a squeal with her hand.

"A date!" Annie leaned across the table with wide eyes, as eager to hear the scoop as Marcy would be, had she been present.

Caroline did a quick sweep of the café to make sure her aunt wasn't lingering nearby and then glared at Valerie. "It wasn't a date."

"She bought a new dress." Valerie casually popped a piece of a blueberry muffin into her mouth.

Eyebrows rose. Looks were exchanged. The consensus seemed to be that it was, indeed, a date.

"I went to a tasting with Lucas Reynolds," Caroline explained with a sigh. "For the wedding. You all know that I'm helping Hillary with her plans."

"Yes, but your dinner wasn't with Hillary. It was with the groom's brother." Again, Val just couldn't keep the glee from her voice.

"Lucas called in a favor with a chef," Caroline said with a shrug. She couldn't meet her sisters' eyes as she reached for her coffee. "Considering my profession and my promise to help Hillary, tasting the food was the least I could do."

"The least you could do!" Annie all but shouted. "Hillary is marrying the man who dumped you at the altar!"

Caroline's gaze darted to a table where two women she vaguely recognized from high school, both a few years older than herself, sat staring at her, their baby strollers parked side by side.

"You know perfectly well that I never even made it to the altar."

"You know what I'm saying." Then, her brow creasing with concern, Annie added, "Look, I didn't say anything when you first mentioned helping with the plans, but I didn't realize just how far you were taking things. Are you really sure that being so involved is such a good idea?"

Caroline didn't answer right away because the truth was that she wasn't sure of anything. She just knew that she was here, in Harmony Cove, and that somehow she'd gotten roped into first being a maid of honor and now a wedding planner for her former fiancé.

And her best friend and cousin.

"You know how much Hillary means to me," she said, feeling the emotions rise up in her voice.

Immediately, Annie backed down. Even Val looked remorseful. Molly stared at the table.

"It's therapeutic, really," Caroline said, only now realizing just how true it was. She felt idle and restless when she considered the lack of work waiting for her back in Philadelphia, and she'd been stressed about returning to her hometown and facing her painful past, but keeping busy left less time for dwelling on any of that.

And, admittedly, more time with Lucas. Who had somehow become more than an ally. Maybe he was even a friend.

"I'm treating this objectively, with professional distance. And in doing so, I've come to realize that I don't have any more feelings for Tim. Not even bad ones, actually."

Well, maybe just a few. But that was to be expected.

"It did seem strange that Hillary didn't have much planned..." Val raised her eyebrows and went back to her muffin.

"But what does Lucas have to do with all of this? I thought you hated him," Annie said.

"Oh..." Caroline tipped her head. "That's a strong word."

Annie's eyes bulged. "Do I need to remind you how he treated you the entire time you and Tim dated? How cold he was to you when you were engaged? How heartless he was when he burst into the room and told you that Tim wouldn't be marrying you after all?"

And again they had the attention of every table in the café.

Not like the entire town hadn't read every dirty detail in Marcy's Harmony Happenings column three years ago. Even Marcy couldn't refrain from publishing that story, though she was kind enough to leave out names.

"Chatting with him when you were stuck sitting beside him at a social gathering is one thing, but going out to dinner just the two of you?" Annie frowned.

"Lucas was the one with the connection," Caroline said.

"Oh, well, isn't that nice of him," Annie said sarcastically. "Where was this burst of generosity three years ago?"

Caroline felt a wave of love for her sister's protectiveness of her. They had a bond, she and Annie, one that Val or Molly couldn't understand. It came from having your heart broken by your first love.

It was the kind of bond that she wouldn't wish on anyone but that she treasured all the same.

"Three years is a long time," she pointed out. "Things happen. People change."

Or they didn't. Because she couldn't be sure that Lucas had changed at all, or if he was the same person he'd always been. Someone she'd never really known.

And if he didn't want Tim to marry her, then why was he pushing so hard for his brother to make it to the altar with Hillary?

"You can say that again," Molly mumbled. "Just look at how much has changed in a matter of months."

"Annie and Sean are back to—wait one moment." Val rummaged in her bag and retrieved today's paper, already opened to the gossip column, which she now scanned as her mouth curved mischievously. "Annie and Sean, not named here, of course, are, and I quote, 'back to whispering behind closed office doors, but it's their moments of silence that are most interesting...'"

Annie gasped loudly while Molly burst out laughing. "Give me that!"

Val held it above her head while Annie reached for it.

"Aren't you the editor?" Caroline asked, also laughing. "You didn't read this before it went to print?"

"That was Sean's job." Annie's mouth thinned, but it was clear she was far from angry when she finally got her hands on the paper and read the article, shaking her head and rolling her eyes as she did so. "Marcy certainly has an overactive imagination."

"Well, you and Sean *are* back together," Caroline pointed out. "As Molly said, a lot has changed recently."

She sighed heavily, and all the sisters seemed to have lost their amusement as the reality of their family situation settled over them. Their father was still holed up in the tiny apartment above the *Harmony Herald* office. Their mother had streaked her hair pink. And worse, she had a new love interest.

"Moving on from your love life to Mom's," Caroline started.

Annie groaned. "Do we have any idea who this mystery man is who has captured our mother's heart?"

"Aren't you supposed to be a reporter?" Valerie tutted.

"Need I remind you that Marcy writes the gossip

column, not me? Besides, I've been busy taking over the paper," Annie insisted.

"Busy doing something," Val said with a waggle of her eyebrows.

Molly giggled, and even Caroline smiled, but she couldn't help but worry about Annie falling hard and fast for Sean again. Who was to say that he wouldn't break her heart all over again, considering that he'd done it so easily once before?

"We really have no idea who this guy is? Even Marcy hasn't spotted them out together?" Caroline asked. There were only so many bachelors of a certain age in this town, and most of them had been married to one of her mother's friends at some point in time.

Her sisters all shook their heads as they sipped their coffee.

"Do you think Dad knows?" Molly asked worriedly, turning her attention to Annie.

"Do you think *he's* bringing a date?" Valerie asked the question that Caroline suspected they were all wondering.

"I'm not sure that he's coming at all," Caroline said sadly, thinking of the RSVPs she'd looked at over the weekend, and the telltale missing one from her father that she'd searched for more than once. But the only additions to the original charts were Lucas's business partners.

Annie drew a long breath. "He doesn't work at the paper anymore so I don't see him every day, but he still pokes his head in from time to time, especially for coffee. And, I think, for company."

They fell silent. They all knew it was their father's way of avoiding coming here to the café.

"He doesn't like to talk about Mom," Annie went on. "I've stopped pressing him about it. It's not my place. But I'm worried now."

"What's he doing now that he's retired?" Caroline asked. "How's he keeping busy?"

Their mother used to joke that the newspaper was his entire life. Caroline wondered if that was part of the reason for their problems, even if she'd never considered it before.

They'd seemed so happy. So in love. So unbreakable.

If they couldn't make it, who could?

"You know Dad," Annie said, her smile returning. "He's not one to stay idle. He's also very private. He's been out and about more than usual, so I know he's up to something. When he's ready, he'll tell us."

"Maybe he's writing a book!" Molly said excitedly.

"It would be just like Dad to do something like write a book about the history of Harmony Cove in his retirement," Valerie agreed.

"Better than the tell-all that his sister would write," Molly said with a snort.

Annie gave a mild smile as she sipped her coffee. "Maybe. Whatever it is, I can't wait to find out."

Caroline wished that she could share her sister's optimism. If their father was acting out of character, then it was entirely possible he was making plans for something that would come as another shock to the family.

And right now, she'd had just about all the heartache she could take for one lifetime.

Caroline left her sisters with the promise to report if she learned anything new about their parents' recent whereabouts, secretly hoping that she didn't. There were some things that were easier not to think about.

Some people, too.

She pushed out into the warm sunshine—and nearly collided with Tim Reynolds. He held out two hands, steadying her by the arms, and the touch was shockingly familiar. But instead of sinking into the feeling or longing for something that had once been so commonplace, Caroline stepped back quickly, nearly stumbling into one of her mother's oversize planters.

Righting herself, she was pleased to see that her coffee hadn't spilled, and even more reassured to notice that, unlike the first time she had an unexpected run-in with this man, her heart wasn't racing with panic.

She studied his features as she would an old photograph, a physical reminder of a time gone by, a moment in her life that had come and gone. It felt nearly impossible to think that once she had enjoyed his touch, kissed that mouth, leaned into that chest.

Somehow it felt much longer than three years ago. Instead of focusing on the last time they saw each other, she was living in the present. And he wasn't a part of it any more than he was her future.

"You're in a good mood this morning," Tim remarked.

"I am," she said, meaning it. Spending time with her sisters had a way of boosting her spirits, even if this morning did remind her of just how much she missed their company.

"You seem to be in quite a hurry for such an early hour," he went on.

Caroline wanted to point out that it was hardly early, but then she remembered that Tim operated on a different schedule than most people. He started his days around ten when he could, nine at best, and stayed out well past most people's bedtimes. When they were dating and Caroline was working at the B&B, she was often ready to turn in by eight, leaving Tim with friends at the bar to walk home alone.

At the time it didn't bother her much. Tim was social, and she was more of a homebody, and they spent plenty of time together.

Only now she knew that it was a red flag she'd overlooked.

She wondered if he left Hillary to walk home alone most nights, and now she supposed he did. Some people changed. Others didn't.

She'd like to think that she fell into the first group, that she'd grown, or at least finally fallen out of love with this man.

But she'd also stopped believing in love, too.

"I was just on my way to meet Hillary to go over the menu for the reception. A highly reputable chef was available for the job last minute." Caroline drew a breath, channeling the professional side of herself, not the woman who had been left heartbroken by the man standing in front of her.

He didn't have any power over her anymore. He couldn't hurt her again. She wouldn't let him.

And she wouldn't let him hurt Hillary, either.

"How's...Philadelphia?" Tim seemed to take a moment to remember where she lived now. Further confirmation of how little he cared.

He'd never tried to track her down. Never looked for her. Never attempted to make things right.

And now here they were, face-to-face, just the two of them, for the first time since the night before their wedding day.

She'd imagined this moment as many times as she feared it, and now that it was here, she found that she no longer cared. Staring into the eyes that she'd looked into every day for years, she no longer saw the man she once thought she'd share her life with. She saw a stranger. A man she didn't know.

And maybe never did.

"It's great," Caroline said with more conviction than she felt. Then, deciding that there was really no need to put on pretenses with this man who had given her so little thought and still didn't, she admitted, "But...it's not Harmony Cove."

Tim's eyes seemed to darken. "Are you thinking of moving back?"

Caroline smiled brightly. "Maybe."

She'd only said it to show Tim that she wasn't going to hide from him forever, but as she said it, she realized that it was true. That maybe she should move back. There was nothing stopping her—there never had been, other than her own wounded heart.

"Hillary said you're quite the event planner," Tim went

on, giving her a strange look, as if trying to make sense of this new life of hers. One that didn't include him and never would.

"I have my own business."

It hurt her to say it, though. She much preferred to have a partner. Even though she'd moved away to be alone, telling herself after what Tim had done to her that life was better lived alone, she knew that wasn't any more true now than it was then.

"No wonder you were able to find a top chef on such short notice," Tim said, giving her a funny smile.

A compliment? She supposed she could take it, but coming from him, she didn't need to.

Besides, it wouldn't be fair.

"What's this I hear about a chef?" Hillary was quickly coming down the sidewalk, her eyes darting from Caroline to Tim and back again.

Caroline gave her cousin a smile to show that everything was fine, just fine. That somehow, she was able to stand on a sidewalk and have a civil conversation with the man who had abandoned her on her wedding day.

That she was over it. Because maybe she really was.

"Caroline found a caterer for the reception," Tim told his bride, reaching out to slip a hand around her waist.

"Lucas pulled some strings, actually." Caroline felt this was a safe comment, and it would surely explain how they were able to get such a renowned chef on short notice.

"He did?" Hillary shook her head, grinning broadly. "But then, of course he did. He's been so supportive ever since the proposal. He even hosted our engagement party."

Caroline couldn't hide her surprise. "*Really?*"

At her own engagement party, Lucas hadn't made a toast. But as Caroline thought back on what Lucas said at dinner, she now knew why.

She just couldn't be sure why this time around he felt differently.

Twelve

The plans for the wedding had come together, and by the time Friday rolled around, Caroline was able to look at her checklist and feel almost satisfied.

As with the other events she'd planned, a true sense of accomplishment would not come until the party was winding down and all the guests were tired and smiling, a sign of a good time if ever there was one.

Only in this case, she knew that she couldn't feel too on top of things, not when so much was ultimately out of her control. It wouldn't matter if the flowers were perfect or the food was delicious if, in the end, there was no one to enjoy it.

No, as with her own wedding, she was powerless against the outcome. Only this time, at least she was prepared.

She just hoped that a tiny part of her cousin was bracing herself, too.

The Sweet Harmony Café closed just after lunch so the family could start preparing for the rehearsal dinner, which was more of a gathering and less of a rehearsal. Caroline showed up just in time to have the last cup of chowder, knowing from experience that it was probably all she'd end up eating for the rest of the day. Even though she was technically a guest at the rehearsal dinner since her mother had undertaken its planning, she wasn't one to sit still, and she had a feeling that her mother would need her help more than she knew if the look of relief when Caroline arrived said anything.

"I don't know how we're going to transform this place in just three hours," Sharon fretted from behind the counter. She began emptying baskets of uneaten muffins into bakery boxes, which Caroline knew Molly would run over to the local community center, where they would be enjoyed by the seniors at their weekly card game.

"But the party doesn't start until six," Molly said as she wiped down the last of the empty tables.

Caroline looked at her mother in confusion until she realized the true source of her mother's anxiety.

This wasn't about the party at all. It was about her date for the party.

And her mother wasn't the only one with butterflies; Caroline's stomach had been fluttering all day when she thought of seeing Lucas. She told herself that she'd gotten used to his company, nothing more, and that it wasn't his company that she'd missed these past few days since their dinner, but his camaraderie. It was nice to spend time with someone who saw the world the way she did, even if that person happened to be her ex's brother.

"I think if we go through the checklist, we can have everything set up by four," Caroline assured her mother.

"That will leave us all plenty of time to go home and get cleaned up and changed."

"Checklist?" Her mother stared blankly, and Caroline was hit with the reminder of just how long three years away was—and how much things could change, and how much they didn't.

And how much could be forgotten.

Her mother was many things—an excellent cook, a knowledgeable gardener, a nurturing caregiver and homemaker, and, once, a loving wife. But when it came to organization, she had her own system. The café's kitchen was cluttered with scribbled lists and stained recipe cards, all in shorthand, all perfectly understood by Sharon Baker and nearly no one else. Caroline's childhood home was mostly the same, delightfully cluttered with mementos collected over the years, not exactly tidy, but lived in, and while it might seem at first glance that nothing had its place, the Baker family had a system.

Caroline had evolved over the years to simply have a more rigid one. One that was her armor against error or mistakes. Or surprises.

Even the good ones, she thought, thinking back to how safe but boring her life had become over the years.

And just how lonely.

"Don't worry, Mom," Caroline said with a smile. "I can quickly put together a list of everything we need to remember to do before the doors open tonight. Place cards set out, flowers on the table, that sort of thing. That way you don't have to worry about forgetting anything."

"In that case, I had better get started on the remaining

appetizers that couldn't be prepped in advance. Delia is staying late to help with service tonight so I can enjoy the party. Will you girls be okay out here without me for a bit?" Sharon looked worried, but Caroline set a reassuring hand on her arm.

"This is what I do for a living, Mom. By the time you reemerge from that kitchen, this entire space will be completely transformed and most of the boxes on my checklist will be ticked."

Seeming satisfied, Sharon grinned and pushed through the swinging door into the kitchen. Caroline brushed a loose strand of hair from her forehead and looked around the space, telling herself not to panic, at least not yet. One step at a time, she reminded herself. They would get it done. They had no choice.

"Speaking of transformation," she said as she grabbed a rag and helped her sister clean the remaining tables. "Molly, do you mind lending me a dress?"

That was one item that hadn't made it onto her checklist and one that she had overlooked in her planning for the night. She knew she could wear the one she'd bought at the boutique for her dinner with Lucas, and she'd intended to do just that, only now...

Now she didn't want to be seen in the same dress twice in one week.

For the first time in years, she wanted to be noticed. To feel special.

And Lucas made her feel just that.

"I have a blue one from a baby shower I went to last

summer," Molly said with a nod. "It will look so pretty with your eyes."

"Not that I'm trying to impress anyone," Caroline said, even though she wasn't so sure that was true. She was trying to feel good about herself, nothing more.

"Not even Lucas?" Molly asked, pausing only to grin. "Not even a little?"

Caroline thought about that for a moment, knowing that Molly's question was innocent rather than teasing or prying. "At first I might have said yes if only because success is the best revenge. But I no longer feel like I have anything to prove to Lucas or even to Tim. Tim is marrying Hillary, and for her sake, I hope he's changed his ways. And Lucas...I don't think he's changed, but I think that I just never really understood him before."

"But you do now," Molly commented. "And...you like him."

"*Like* is a strong word." Only she couldn't deny that she did like him. More than a little, and much more than she ever expected to.

"Not as strong as *love*," Molly said in a singsong voice that pulled a grin from Caroline.

"And what about you?" Caroline asked as they began pushing the tables together to form longer seating arrangements. Caroline's mother had ordered the flowers and candles ahead of time, and they planned to line the lengths with votives and small bundles of mixed bouquets; given the low inventory at the flower shop, it was the perfect way to brighten up the space and use up what was still available.

"Oh, I'll find something to wear," Molly said with a shrug.

"I mean, is there anyone special that you're looking forward to seeing tonight?" Caroline prodded.

Across the table, Molly's cheeks turned pink, but she shook her head. "No," she said with a sigh. "And I suppose it's just as well. I'm so busy here at the café. Mom needs my help more than ever now that she's..." She stopped to gulp. "Dating."

Caroline's stomach knotted on the word, but she pushed the thought away quickly. There was a long list of things to do to make this cozy space look elegant, and even three sets of hands would make that a challenge given that their mother would be mostly busy in the kitchen.

The tables out front on the sidewalk would be moved to the side patio, a slightly more intimate area walled in by thick hedges that was going to be used for the cocktail hour and conversation area. It was amazing what some white tablecloths, candlelight, and flowers could do to a space.

After forty-five minutes, some rearranging, and a final count of chairs, the dining space of the café looked completely different. Instead of tables scattered around the room, three long tables ran perpendicular to the counter, the head table backing up to the open doors to the side patio. The opposite wall would be used for a buffet station, so Sharon wouldn't have to worry about serving anyone, and the main counter would be used for drinks. Another bar cart would be set up on the patio so guests could serve themselves. It would be a casual event, relaxed and welcoming.

The last night before the big day.

Caroline couldn't help but worry on Hillary's behalf, knowing how her own rehearsal dinner had felt so jovial and cozy, too, only to take a stark turn the very next day.

"Why don't we go get the flowers?" she suggested before her thoughts got the better of her. The flower shop was only a block away, and between the two of them, they could get everything back in one trip. "I could use some fresh air."

"Me, too," Molly said, her eyes suddenly searching Caroline. "Are you sure that you're going to be okay, Caroline? You can tell me. I know you've been strong, but now that the wedding day is nearly here..."

"It's fine," Caroline said. They stepped into the sunshine and she breathed in the salty air. "*I'm* fine."

More than fine, really. And it had nothing to do with Tim or this wedding. It was about being here, in Harmony Cove, with the sea air in her face, and her sister at her side.

And, as much as she didn't want to admit it, the promise of seeing Lucas in just a few hours. Lucas, who it turned out had liked her all along. Who thought that she was too good for his brother.

Who had her best interest at heart.

Just like she had her cousin's.

"I hate to say it, but I'm worried that Hillary is not fine, or won't be, in the end," she sighed, knowing that she could confide with Molly and hoping that her aunt Marcy wasn't lingering in a shop doorway or behind one of the many trees that lined Water Street.

"Oh, I'd say that everyone's a little anxious and no one will admit it." Molly sighed. "I'd hate to see Hillary as hurt as you were, Caroline, but at the same time, I have to admit that I don't want to see that man happy, either."

Caroline tucked her arm around Molly's waist. "I know the feeling. For years, I've hoped that Tim's life would end in misery. But if Hillary's happiness rides on his, then who am I to blame them for it? Besides, I'm over Tim."

And she was. She really, truly was.

Feeling better than she had in weeks, she pushed into the storefront of the flower shop, which looked particularly leaner than it had just a few days ago. It saddened Caroline to think of such a beloved local store shuttering, and she was happy to have an excuse to give Sheila all the business she could in its final days.

"So, what has you feeling so much better about things with Tim?" Molly asked once they were back outside, each holding a box containing six small arrangements.

"I guess I always thought I'd move on quicker if I didn't have to be reminded of him all the time, but that just kept the last memory of him alive and present. Now that I've faced this town again—and him—I realize that all those feelings I thought I still had were just in my head. Not my heart. Tim hasn't had a place there for a very long time."

"And does someone else hold that place now?" Molly asked coyly as they approached the café.

Caroline pushed the door open with her hip and gave Molly a stern look. "You sound like Val. Has she been filling your ears with nonsense?"

Molly gave a knowing smile but said nothing. "I'm just saying that it wouldn't be so bad to find love again, would it?"

No, Caroline thought, it wouldn't. But she still wasn't so sure that such a thing existed. For her.

Or, she thought, looking over at her mother, who was setting up the votive candles, for anyone.

The women arrived back at the café just in time for the first guests to arrive. Caroline's cousins arrived as a group, including Paige, who had driven in from Boston, followed soon after by Annie and Sean, holding hands, and looking every bit as relaxed with each other as they had ten years ago.

Caroline set the final place card on the table and turned to her mother, who was flushed in the cheeks, her green eyes bright as they darted to the door.

"You look really nice, Mom," Caroline said, as much as it hurt to think of the reasons behind it. "And you've done a great job with the place. It looks beautiful."

And it did. The tables were covered in small arrangements and candles, the waning sunlight lent a glow to the room, and outside on the patio, the strings of lights and soft music were inviting.

"I think we're only waiting on the bride and groom," Caroline said, knowing just how weird that sounded.

"And one more," her mother said with a sly smile.

Oh, no. Not another one who was suggesting that Caroline had something going on with Lucas. Caroline was about to protest when she felt her mother's hand on her arm.

"And here is my date now."

So he had come tonight, just like she and her sisters had

feared. Caroline's heart dropped into her stomach, and she turned to the door that her mother was walking toward, but her dread was quickly replaced with shock.

There was a man standing in the doorway, wearing a navy blazer and khaki pants, and a shy smile that still managed to crinkle the corners of his warm blue eyes.

But the man wasn't just any man. It was Caroline's father.

"Dad? But..." But her words were lost with the background music, and her mother wasn't listening anyway. Mitch stood at the door, his eyes on only one woman in the room, not that Caroline felt slighted, not in the least.

With tears brimming in her eyes, she watched in awe as her father presented his wife with a single flower, and then took her arm and led her over to the refreshment stand. Across the room, Caroline felt Annie's stare, and they both exchanged the same elated grin, one that was quickly joined by Val and Molly, who was blatantly wiping away tears with the back of her hand.

Even Sandra looked genuinely happy for her sister, considering that she'd officially lost her happy hour buddy.

Caroline blinked back tears of astonishment and joy as she watched her parents clink glasses and then each take a sip of champagne, and her heart felt fuller than it had in months. Maybe even years.

She thought she'd planned everything for this wedding. The flowers, the food, even the possibility of the groom being another no-show.

But somehow, life still managed to slip in a surprise. And this time, a good one.

She was still smiling when she walked out onto the patio, just as Lucas was coming up the road, wearing a navy suit and a striped tie, his brown hair tousled in the wind. His expression lifted when he spotted her, and his face broke out into a smile, one that reached all the way up to those eyes, and from the way her chest swelled, she knew that she had been wrong just now, that her heart wasn't fuller than it had ever been.

But it was now.

"A toast," Lucas said after procuring them two glasses. They were tucked away in a corner of the patio, and most of the guests were still inside, finishing the delicious cupcakes that Kathy and Lucy had made for the dessert.

Caroline held her glass to his. "To pulling it off."

"I was going to say to *almost* pulling it off." Lucas's grin was wry. "We still have to get through tomorrow."

"And I'll be wearing a large turquoise dress for that," Caroline said with a laugh, determined to keep the mood light, and not to let Tim, or even her concern for her cousin, ruin what had turned out to be one of the best evenings she'd had in too long. They clinked glasses and she took a sip of the cold, bubbly liquid, finally letting herself relax.

The party was a success. The food was, not surprisingly, delicious, and everyone seemed to be in a good mood, especially Caroline's parents, who were still sitting side by side at their table, sipping coffee, well past the end of the dessert course.

"It's almost enough to make you believe in love," Caroline said as she watched them through the open door, lost in thought. Her cheeks heated when she felt Lucas staring at her. "Sorry. I know that's not your thing."

"I was just going to say the same thing," he said with a slow grin.

She blinked at him as her heart started to speed up. "Really? But..."

There was a loud noise from inside, and then a burst of laughter as Tim and Travis caught the attention of half the group.

Lucas fixed his gaze through the window on Tim in a way that made Caroline stiffen a little, bringing her back to her own rehearsal dinner.

"You're still worried about tomorrow?" She knew that as Tim's brother, he must have the best read on the situation.

"Don't worry," Lucas assured her, giving her a small smile that did little to make her feel better on Hillary's behalf. "I'm not going to let my brother make a mistake again."

"Honestly, in a way you spared me," Caroline assured him.

Lucas frowned at her. "Really? But I thought you hated me for what I did."

"I did," Caroline admitted. Now it was her turn to give him a small smile. "But I see now that you did me a favor. The only thing worse than being left at the altar is being married to the wrong man. Tim didn't love me. If he did, he wouldn't have put me through that. If he did, he would have at least had the courage to tell me himself instead of sending you."

"But that's where you're wrong." Lucas firmed his mouth. "Sorry, I've said too much."

Caroline's heart tripped. "No, I want to hear it. Please." Or at least she needed to hear the missing part of her past that she'd never understood.

Lucas huffed out a breath and looked directly at her. His usually intense eyes were soft, filled with something that seemed an awful lot like an apology. When he spoke, he lowered his voice, even though they were well out of earshot, and everyone else was fully engrossed in their own conversations.

"Tim didn't send me that day, Caroline. He didn't ask me to speak to you. He just disappeared. I tried calling him but he had his phone turned off. I waited until I didn't think I could wait any longer, and in the end, I had to face the truth. And share it with you." His expression clouded over. "I'm sorry, Caroline. I never wanted to deliver that message. But I felt like you deserved to hear it. You deserved more than no words at all."

Caroline felt lightheaded, and she dropped onto the nearest chair, needing to process what Lucas had just told her, and the events of that day that she had replayed over and over again for weeks and months, trying to make sense of it.

"He went to Boston," Lucas said, quickly pulling up a seat beside her. "I didn't see him again for months. Didn't speak to him, either. When we did, it was just about business."

"So he never told you why he changed his mind?" Caroline needed to know if only to fill in the gaps of a story she'd told herself.

Lucas shook his head. "You know Tim."

"Does anyone know Tim?" Caroline replied. She glanced over her shoulder into the café, where Hillary was barely visible, looking happy and relaxed as she chatted with family. She turned back to Lucas. "Thank you. For telling me. Tonight. And...that day."

"I kicked myself about it for months," Lucas admitted, his shoulders relaxing under his blazer. "I wish I had been less matter-of-fact, but I didn't understand, myself. I just knew that Tim wasn't coming. And I knew that I had to tell you. And that was all I could tell you. The facts, not the reason behind them. I couldn't offer you more than that."

Caroline nodded. "I understand." She understood his part in that day, at least.

And in the days before it.

"There's just one thing I don't understand," she said, looking up into his dark eyes. "How can you support this wedding but not mine?"

"Are you asking if I think Hillary can do better?" Lucas gave her a long look that sent butterflies through Caroline's stomach. "I'd like to think that Tim has learned. That he's changed. That he won't make the same mistake twice."

"Does anyone really change, though?" Caroline asked.

"I think I have," Lucas said, locking her gaze.

Caroline tipped her head, even as she considered her own journey. She'd gone from being that heartbroken girl who was afraid to show her face in her hometown to a woman who could not only plan her ex-fiancé's wedding but also hope that it was a success.

Maybe it was growth. Or maybe it was time.

Or maybe it was the man sitting beside her, giving her a look that she'd seen before, all those years ago. One so intense she'd assumed it was dislike.

When she couldn't have more wrong.

"That comment you made just now. About love not being my thing..."

"Yes?" Her voice came out in a whisper.

"It wasn't. It never felt like it could be. Not when I've witnessed what love can do to a person. I always thought it led to pain, but lately, I've been thinking that I could be wrong. About love. About it not being for me."

Her heart started to race as his gaze held hers, the intensity that once felt judgmental now becoming a connection, a bond that she didn't want to break and that maybe he didn't, either.

"You can't be sure of anything, though." As soon as she said it, she wished she could take it back, along with the last three years that she'd spent hiding from her pain. Her family. And love.

She wanted to go back and open her heart. And believe. In love. And all its sweet possibilities.

She waited for him to nod, to confirm what he'd already said, a sentiment that they had shared.

Until now.

Instead, his mouth lifted into a smile. "I can be sure that I won't let you down, Caroline. I can be sure of that."

Her heart soared and swooped and before she could

overthink it, or remind herself of everything that could go wrong, of all the unpredictable parts of life that were out of her control, he took her hand and pulled her behind the row of hedges, his face so close to hers that she could feel the heat of his body nearly pressing against her own. He leaned in and teased her mouth with his lips, gently, slowly, until she folded under the warmth of his arms, forgetting that anyone might see them, just like she forgot all her worries and woes, and what had brought her to this point.

And she let herself fall. For Lucas. For love. And for the hope that only it could bring.

Thirteen

Lucas stood stiffly in his best man suit near the door of his apartment, checking his watch for the eleventh time in twenty minutes, only relaxing for the first time that morning when he heard the knock at his door.

"About time!" He could hear the relief in his voice but his smile faded when he saw the look on Tim's face.

A look he had seen before. A look that he never wanted to see again.

"I have your suit," Lucas said, stepping back to let his brother inside. His head was spinning but he tried to maintain an air of calm, hoping that if he could get Tim past the jitters, then they could get on with the day as planned.

Tim said nothing as he walked over to the couch and sat down.

Lucas drew a steadying breath and went to the lone armchair he owned, facing his brother. His apartment was comfortable but made for one. One bedroom. One armchair. Heck, he didn't even have a dining room table. He ate on a barstool at the kitchen counter on the nights he wasn't heating up a microwavable meal to eat at his desk on the construction site.

Up until recently, working through dinner didn't bother him any more than his barely functional and hardly lived-in personal space. But now he knew that despite what he'd told himself was true, there was more to life than the business or even the hotel.

And he wanted more. Much as it scared him to admit it.

He could blame his bland apartment on not being back in town for long—but his condo in Boston was the same. He used to see nothing wrong with this way of life. Now, he saw everything wrong with it.

It was a place that didn't see much company. When he met his friends, which wasn't often, it was at a bar in town. The few dates he ever had were out, and even if he brought women back for a night, it was never for a future.

And that was the problem with this apartment. It was a place to live. A place he was stuck. In the present. In the past.

But not in the future.

And he'd come back to Harmony Cove to make a life for himself. Not just build a hotel. He just hadn't realized that the two were separate until recently.

"What's up?" He kept his tone light, even though his stomach was tight with anxiety. Tim looked pale, and it didn't take a genius to know that Lucas's fear was coming true.

"I don't think I can do this," Tim said, his voice barely audible.

Even though Lucas had been bracing himself for this, it

still came as a blow. He closed his eyes, picturing Wallace Hadley, probably already taking his seat at the ceremony.

"Sure you can." Lucas forced a grin. "Today is no different than yesterday, or the day before. You love Hillary. And she loves you."

"See that's just the thing," Tim said, looking him dead in the eye now. "I'm not sure that's true."

Lucas tried to fight his frown. "I've seen the two of you together."

He didn't add that their interactions made him wary, and not for the same reasons he'd had when Tim was dating Caroline. To the best of his knowledge, his brother had been faithful to Hillary, but he didn't light up in her presence the way he once had with Caroline.

A miserable thought took hold even as Lucas struggled to accept it. Was his original concern founded? Was Tim still in love with his childhood sweetheart?

"Then surely you've noticed that something is off," Tim said bluntly.

"Maybe it's jitters," Lucas suggested. "Ever think of that?"

Tim chewed his lip. He didn't look convinced.

"If you weren't sure you wanted to get married, then you never should have proposed in the first place," Lucas ground out, feeling his long-suppressed anger rise to the surface. He'd kept quiet, all this time, telling himself it was for the best that Tim had bailed on Caroline, even though he'd been cruel to drag things out as long as he did. But now he couldn't keep his feelings inside any longer. Hillary was a sweet person, someone who had accepted Tim's proposal and was planning to start her life with him today.

And Caroline...Caroline was special. Kind, funny, and generous.

Tim's eyebrows shot up in surprise, but he nodded. "Are you talking about Hillary...or Caroline?"

"Both?" Lucas glared at his brother. "Does it matter?"

"I'm just saying that you've gotten awfully close to Caroline these past few days."

"And why should that bother you? You treated her badly, Tim. She's a great woman and you took her for granted. You cheated on her. Repeatedly. And then you didn't even have the guts to tell her you didn't want to marry her. So why do you suddenly care about her now?"

Now it was Tim who did the glaring.

"Hillary is the woman you should care about," Lucas reminded him.

"I do," Tim said. "But...I just don't think I care about her enough to make it last. I think I got swept up in the moment."

Lucas wasn't buying it. "You're far from a romantic, Tim. If you were, then you'd have stopped to do one nice thing for either of these women, like say, plan your honeymoon, which I am now guessing you never did because deep down you knew all along that you weren't going through with this wedding."

Tim didn't respond, which only confirmed what Lucas already knew.

"And you mean to tell me that last night wasn't you

doing the same? Getting caught up with a pretty woman, and the ambiance of the romantic environment?"

So Tim had seen the kiss, or gotten wind of it, at least. Lucas set his jaw, refusing to admit that it was, even as he questioned it himself. It had been a gorgeous night, and Caroline was a beautiful woman. He'd let his emotions get the better of him; the walls he'd put in place had finally come down, against all his judgment and apprehension. He'd given in, but he hadn't gotten swept up.

Lucas wasn't like Tim. He thought things through. He planned. He didn't take anything for granted. Or lightly.

"Why get engaged?" he demanded, refusing to let his brother turn the conversation onto him. "Why propose at all?"

Tim blinked a few times as if searching for the answer. "With Caroline, it was the natural order of things. We'd dated for so long, it was what came next, even if I didn't want it to ever come at all. And then with Hillary, I guess there was some level of redemption involved. I saw the way everyone looked at me when I came back to town to work on the hotel project. I thought that this was my chance to show the Bakers, and the town, that I'm not who they all think I am. But the thing is that I am who they think I am, Lucas. I guess…I wanted to believe that I could have something different than what we had growing up, but deep down, I know that it's just not in me. It's not who I am. I tried to fight it, Lucas, honestly, I did, but I can't make myself be someone I'm not. And…I'm not the marrying kind."

"Isn't it a little late to just be figuring this out?" Lucas ground out. "People are expecting you, Tim. Hillary. Her family."

"Wallace Hadley? Steve?" Tim raised an eyebrow. "Don't think I didn't know what you were doing, Lucas. Why you cared so much about this wedding being successful. Enough to find a caterer for the reception."

Enough to spend time with Caroline Baker.

Enough to write check after check.

"This was never about my future," Tim said angrily. "This was about the future of the company. So before you get on your high horse and say that if I don't go through with today I'm just like Dad, then maybe you should look in the mirror. I may be like him when it comes to my love life, but when it comes to business, that's all you."

Lucas pulled back, feeling the weight of his brother's words, and, much as he didn't like them, knowing that they were true.

"Have you really thought about what you'd be doing?" Lucas said in a low voice, trying to bring some calm back to the conversation. To right at least one wrong.

"For Hillary? Or the company?" Tim shot back.

Lucas briefly closed his eyes. "Both. There are consequences for every action, Tim."

"You think I don't know that?" Tim shook his head. "A little credit would be nice for once."

"Credit?" Lucas couldn't stop his voice from rising. "You want me to pat you on the back for breaking Caroline's heart?"

"I loved Caroline as much as I've ever loved anyone,"

Tim replied, his tone sobering. "But maybe I'll never love anyone enough to make that sort of commitment."

Lucas swallowed hard on that, still picturing the hurt in Caroline's eyes when he'd delivered the news that awful day. He'd wanted to punch his brother, and it had probably been for the best that Tim had laid low until things calmed down.

And now, he felt like punching him again.

Lucas bristled, then raked a hand through his hair, not caring if he mussed it. What did it matter now when there would be no wedding unless he managed to convince his brother that love was real, and love could last?

Something he hadn't even believed himself.

Until this past week.

"If you weren't ready for a commitment then you never should have made one," he said, trying to temper his anger.

"I thought it was nerves," Tim said. "But I know that it wasn't."

"And how do you know that?" Lucas asked in frustration.

"Because I didn't miss her," Tim said with a heavy sigh. "I mean, I missed the old times, when we were young, but I didn't regret what I did, only how I did it. I didn't reach out to her, not because I was ashamed of what I'd done, but because I didn't want to try to win her back, and I didn't want her to get the wrong impression. I may be a coward, but I'm not completely heartless."

Lucas stayed quiet. He still wasn't convinced.

"And when I saw you kiss her last night...I didn't feel anything," Tim said with a sigh. He picked at an imaginary string on his pants. "Maybe I'm not capable of feeling anything for anyone, not to the depth that I should, at least."

"Not even Hillary?" Lucas asked after a heavy pause.

"With Hillary, it was different than it ever was with Caroline. For the first time, I was dating as an adult, not as a kid, you know? Sure, we'd always known each other, but not in that way. It was new and exciting, whereas with Caroline it was warm and familiar."

Warm. Familiar. Lucas still didn't see the problem there. If anything, it sounded pretty wonderful.

"I thought that meant that I was on the right path. That this was what love was. That this was made to last." Tim looked pleadingly at him. "But I don't think what Hillary and I ever had was love. I think we were both getting to a certain age, looking for company, and happy to have found it for a while."

Lucas stared at his brother until he couldn't anymore and then sank his head into his hands. He wished that they had an aunt or an uncle, someone other than two parents who had been a wretched example of marriage, who might shed some light and set Tim straight. Explain to him what love really was, and how you knew it was meant to last.

Explain to them both, because Lucas didn't know any more than Tim did.

And maybe he should stop blaming his brother for that.

"You know what your reputation is in this town," Lucas finally said. "You know what's at stake."

They both did. And for Tim, it was so much more than the business.

But this wedding wasn't just about his brother, Lucas knew. It was also about Hillary.

"I know exactly what's at stake," Tim finally said, breaking the silence that had been filled with a dozen thoughts, and none of them good. "But you and I both know what happens to people who get married when they shouldn't."

Visions of their parents screaming in the kitchen made Lucas clench his teeth. He nodded because it still hurt too much to speak about it.

"Mom once told me that she tried to back out, the night before her wedding to Dad, but that her parents threatened to cut her off if she did. Their parents were friends. It was a status thing. A different time…"

Lucas stiffened in surprise. "She told you that?"

Tim nodded. "After my first wedding. She was trying to be supportive, but it made me think about why she and Dad always fought so much. They forced something, Lucas. What they had was never love."

It was never love. Lucas sat with this, replaying his childhood with this new information. All this time, he'd thought that his parents had simply fallen out of love when the truth was that they'd never found it in the first place.

Releasing a steady breath, Lucas stared at his kid brother, the very one whom he'd taken out to toss the ball when their parents' shouting grew too loud. He'd tried so hard to shield him from pain, and even now, all these years later, he knew he still would.

"Are you sure?" he asked. "Do you want to take a few

minutes, half an hour even, to think about it? Or do you want to call Hillary, just to...check in?"

Tim shook his head. "I've been thinking about it all night. All week even. And I came to one conclusion. If I were to get married today, I'd be doing it for all the wrong reasons. Hillary doesn't deserve that."

"No," Lucas replied quietly. "She doesn't."

No one did.

Caroline stood in Hillary's childhood bedroom, the same one where they'd spent so many Saturday nights giggling long into the night, or later, lying on the bed, flipping through magazines, dreaming about their future selves.

But the future was now.

The ceremony seating was set up along the bay, and so was the tent for the reception. Caroline had personally helped Sheila deliver the flowers, and now she had to fight the tears in her eyes, and it had nothing to do with the fact that try as Aunt Sandra might, her bridesmaid dress was still a full size too small in the chest and might be cutting off the circulation in her abdomen.

Hillary stood before the mirror they'd once shared to experiment with makeup and hairstyles, looking radiant in her simple white gown while her mother clipped the dramatic veil onto her head. Her jewelry was simple: pearl earrings that matched the embellishment on the clasp of the veil that rested on her low bun, a nod to the seaside wedding.

"Do you feel like today is the happiest day of your life?" Sandra asked.

Hillary blinked a few times and then nodded. Caroline saw her wipe away a tear and she did the same. If someone had asked her just three years to imagine a time when she would be fluffing the veil for Tim's bride, she'd have laughed out loud and then burst into tears, but right now, knowing the bride, and loving her as she did, she could only hope for the best.

Her eyes went to the clock on Hillary's bedside table, as it had every minute since they'd arrived. Each second that passed was a good sign. Soon, they would all pile into Sandra's classic Cadillac, one that she'd had detailed especially for today, and drive over to the beach. Today was Hillary's wedding day, not hers. And today would be different. It would be happy. It would be the start of a future that Caroline wasn't meant to have.

Even if it had taken until now to realize that.

The doorbell rang, and Sandra swooped her hands to her chest. "That'll be some of the girls," she said as she disappeared into the hall, her voice growing distant as she hurried down the stairs. "We're leaving soon, so don't dawdle!"

Hillary gave an eye roll. "She thinks I'm still twelve."

"*I* think you're still twelve," Caroline said with a laugh. She looked around the room wistfully, still painted a pale shade of blue with white trim, just like her own childhood bedroom. "Being back here makes me feel like time stood still."

"I miss our sleepovers," Hillary said sadly. "It's strange to think that there will never be another one."

"Oh, now, don't say that..." Caroline chided, but with change came loss. She felt it, too.

"How can I not? Starting today, I'll be spending every night for the rest of my life with Tim," Hillary said, and not exactly happily. "The days of movie marathons and ice cream with saltines and giggling through face masks are over. Oh, Caroline, I wish you hadn't moved away. I wish... Well, I wish so many things."

Tears filled Hillary's eyes, and Caroline hurried to squeeze her hand before they fell and messed up her makeup.

"I know," Caroline whispered, getting choked up herself. "But it's all right now. Everything's going to be okay."

Only right now, she had the very uneasy feeling that this wasn't the case.

Something was amiss here, with the bride, with the energy of the house. It was as if a hush had fallen over the entire world until a pounding was heard on the wooden stairs.

"Hillary?" Sandra was back, only her earlier excitement was gone, and her skin looked pale, her eyes too wide. She stepped aside as another person appeared behind her, only it wasn't Annie or Molly or one of Hillary's sisters.

It was a man in a suit.

It was Lucas.

Lucas met her eyes as he came to stand in the doorway, and Caroline knew from the dread she saw pass through them what he was about to say. She froze, starting to shake, unable to accept that the worst moment of her life was happening all over again, only not to her this time—but to someone she loved.

He turned behind him, muttering something, and more footsteps could be heard slowly approaching.

Caroline threw Hillary a desperate look, but Hillary was still staring at the door, this time as Tim appeared, looking more than a little reluctant and wearing jeans and a rumpled T-shirt.

Looking like a man who had no intention of being at the altar in thirty minutes.

"Do you want me to stay?" Caroline whispered, setting a hand on Hillary's arm.

Hillary stood perfectly still, as pretty as a picture in her beautiful handmade gown and veil, her hair styled and makeup perfectly applied. The earlier tears had dried up, and when she turned to Caroline, she seemed to be in a state of resignation.

"I'll be okay," Hillary said with a small smile.

Caroline wished she could believe that. She glared at Tim, whose shoulders hunched as she pushed past him and out of the room to where Lucas was now standing in the hallway, his hands plunged into his pants pockets, his eyelids heavy.

"Let's go downstairs," Caroline said, hurrying down the stairs in her bare feet. Sandra was already in the kitchen on the phone with her hand covering the mouthpiece, no doubt talking to Kathy or Caroline's mother.

She opened the front door, Lucas close behind her, and started to pace.

"I can't believe this!" she cried, whipping around to stare at Lucas for some sort of explanation, even though she knew that wasn't fair. "But then, I should, huh? The guy makes promises and he breaks them. He doesn't care who he hurts. Did he ever even love Hillary? Did he ever—" She stopped herself. She and Tim were history. Besides, she knew the answer.

Tim had never loved her. You didn't do this to someone you loved.

She gripped the porch rail and stared out onto the lush green lawn edged with the first hydrangea blooms of the season, their petals as blue as the cloudless sky.

It was a beautiful day for a wedding. But, just like her day three years ago, there wouldn't be a wedding after all.

"I tried to talk him into it," Lucas said as he came to stand beside her, looking visibly distressed. He raked his hand through his already tousled hair, sending it astray.

"Well, at least he's willing to tell Hillary in person," Caroline said with a bitter laugh. She shook her head, her blood rushing with anger when she considered what was happening in that bedroom right now. The fallout. The tears. The heartache that she knew all too well.

"He's being responsible," Lucas said with a nod.

Caroline stopped walking to stare at him. "*Responsible*?" she cried. "He's breaking up with yet another woman. On his wedding day."

"Isn't that better than breaking up with her afterward?" Lucas said.

Caroline gaped at him, momentarily speechless. "You *approve* of this?"

"You said yourself that he did you a favor!" Lucas insisted.

Caroline blinked. Had she said that? Not in those words, and only in hindsight. It hardly erased the pain that Tim had caused her—or now, Hillary.

"You think he's doing Hillary a favor right now?" Caroline pointed her finger to the shingled house behind her. "Hillary is in her wedding dress. That her mother made. She spent the morning with her cousins and sisters, getting her hair and nails done. We spent the past week creating a beautiful wedding for her. For them both."

Lucas raised his eyebrows before dropping his head.

She took a steadying breath to calm herself. This wasn't her wedding day. Or her disappointment. She had to remember her place. She was the bride's cousin. Her best friend.

And Lucas had become a friend, too.

Maybe more than one.

"I'm sorry," she said. "You had nothing to do with this."

Lucas closed his eyes, and when he opened them, there was a pained expression she hadn't seen since he'd walked into that room of the church.

Her heart dropped like a stone.

"What's going on?" she said now, as she had then, with dread.

And knowing, even before he spoke.

"He asked for my blessing not to go through with the wedding," Lucas said quietly. "And...I gave it to him."

She stared at him as the shock hit her in waves, harder

than the roughest days in the ocean, the kind where they told you to stay out of the water.

She'd been so careful all these years. Stayed cautious. Protected herself.

Until this past week, when she'd dared to believe in the man standing before her, who'd once again made a fool out of her.

She brushed past him, shaking off his hand as he reached for her. She couldn't even look at him as she hurried down the porch steps and onto the stone path, cutting across the lawn as best she could in these ridiculous shoes that would have been miserable in the sand.

What had Hillary been thinking when she chose these for all the women?

But maybe that was it. Maybe Hillary hadn't been thinking. Not with her head, at least.

She'd been led by her heart. Just like Caroline. And for the second time, they'd been left heartbroken by Reynolds men.

And for the second time, Caroline would be damned if she let one of them see it.

Fourteen

It was nearly evening by the time Caroline finished talking to all of the vendors, explaining the situation, reliving her own heartache when one of them commented on Tim making a habit of this, and handling the necessary donations for the flowers (the nearby hospital and seniors' homes) and cake (to be repurposed into several hundred cake pops to be sold at Kathy's granddaughter's school bake sale on Monday).

It had been a welcome distraction for a few hours, but now as she stood and stretched her back, the emotions hit her full force. She wandered from the porch where she'd been curled up on the porch swing and into the kitchen in search of wine. Her sisters were already waiting for her, gathered around the old wooden table, their bridesmaid dresses swapped out for sweats. Val extended a glass of sauvignon blanc.

"Thanks," Caroline said, dropping into her usual chair, across from Annie, beside Molly.

"How are you doing?" Annie asked cautiously.

"It wasn't my wedding day today," Caroline replied simply. She took a long sip of the chilled white wine, feeling a little better now that she was in her sisters' company. The very comfort she had run from all those years ago.

"I didn't mean about Tim," Annie said. Her look was strangely suggestive.

"I can't believe Lucas would support his brother after this!" Val nearly spat.

Caroline had told them all the details when she'd run back to the house that afternoon. By then, Aunt Sandra had already called her sisters, and the news had spread. No doubt by the morning, it would be in the Harmony Happenings column, with Marcy's dramatic spin, of course.

"You'd managed to convince me he was a good guy," Valerie continued.

Caroline pulled in a breath and released it slowly. She'd managed to convince herself of that, too.

What a fool she'd been. Not once, but twice, when she'd been so careful never to put herself in that position again.

"I should have listened to my gut," Caroline told her sisters. Only, the thing was that she had, hadn't she? She'd tried to ignore her head, instead, the part of her that kept warning her away from him, reminding him of all the times he'd been chilly and cold, even downright rude. But her gut, like her heart, told her that there was more to Lucas than she'd first thought.

That he was worth a second chance. That maybe love was too.

So much for that.

"What will you do now?" Molly asked Caroline. "I

mean, are you still planning to go back to Philadelphia tomorrow or will you stick around a bit for Hillary?"

Caroline wasn't quite ready to respond. Her real reason for coming home had been to check on her family, but after last night, it was clear that her parents were going to be just fine.

It was herself she was less sure about.

"Oh, look at this sight!" Sharon appeared in the doorway, wearing her old flannel robe, her face scrubbed and glowing, her hair pulled back loosely at her neck. She had a book in her hands—her go-to method for relaxation—and, Caroline imagined, a bath running upstairs. "I could get used to seeing all four of my girls under this roof again."

The sisters exchanged a glance, and Caroline knew that everyone was waiting for her to reply. "I won't be away for so long next time," she promised.

But the truth was that she didn't want to leave at all. The old Caroline might have felt the need to run from this latest heartbreak, but she wasn't the same girl who had been left in a beautiful wedding dress with no wedding to be had. She'd gone out into the world, she'd built a business, one she enjoyed, even if it wasn't exactly secure, and she'd come to discover what really mattered.

And it was the people in this room. Her sisters. Her mother. Her father, who she was sure would be moving back into the homestead in due time.

And Hillary.

"I could get used to *all* of us being in the house together again." Molly gave her mother a hopeful look. "Are you and Dad really back together?"

Their mother's smile turned shy for a telling moment. "I hope you girls aren't mad for us keeping this from you. In a town this small, where everyone knows everything, we just... needed some time. Away from each other. And then, with each other. Just the two of us."

Caroline pulled in a breath, catching her sisters' nodding heads. Like them, she understood, even if the thought of her parents splitting up had been torturous.

Everyone needed some space sometimes from the people they loved.

"Have you talked to Sandra?" Caroline asked her mother anxiously. "How's Hillary?"

"Ask her yourself," Sharon replied. "She's at the door."

The sisters exchanged glances, but it was Annie who stood first. "We'll go and let you two talk."

Caroline gave her a smile of thanks. She knew that Annie understood that this wasn't just about Caroline and Hillary having always been close. It was about the bond they now shared, just the two of them.

Caroline walked out into the hallway, unsure of what she would find, only knowing what a wreck she must have looked like in the hours following her own broken engagement. She expected to see swollen, puffy, red-rimmed eyes. A wad of wet tissues clutched in Hillary's hand. Sweats. Maybe even pajamas.

Instead, Hillary still wore a bit of her wedding day makeup, but she'd changed her hair to a neat low ponytail. She wore faded jeans and a lightweight sweater to shield the evening breeze. And she was smiling.

Not a big, toothy smile. But it was there.

Still, that didn't stop Caroline from swooping in to give her a tight hug, releasing her only when Hillary started to laugh.

"It's okay, Caroline, really." Hillary blew out a long breath and then tipped her head to the door. "Want to take a walk? I didn't get to the beach today after all."

"How can you joke about this?" Caroline said, aghast.

Hillary said nothing as she opened the door. Caroline slipped on her flip-flops and joined her. It had cooled off in the time since she'd joined her sisters in the kitchen and she folded her arms against the evening chill, a reminder that the sun was setting, the day was done, and that it hadn't gone as planned.

Or as hoped.

They took the familiar path to the bay, both kicking off their sandals when they reached the sand. Caroline felt her spirits lift as the salt air whipped at her hair, and she didn't even bother to push it from her face.

"Do you want to talk about it?" Caroline asked Hillary as they walked toward the water, dipping their toes in to test the temperature.

"Yes and no." Hillary looked out onto the horizon for a moment and then turned back to her. "I feel terrible."

"Of course you do!" Caroline gushed, setting a hand on her cousin's arm.

"No," Hillary said, shaking her head. "About everything you did to give me a beautiful wedding. Even after what I did. You still showed up for me. And I..."

"You did nothing!" Caroline said firmly. "This was Tim's

decision. Tim's fault." The only mistake that Hillary had made was falling for his charms.

Something she'd done herself.

"But that's just it," Hillary said, giving her a pleading look. "It wasn't his fault, not this time. Tim never should have proposed to me, sure, but I never should have accepted. I never really loved him, I just got...caught up."

Caroline listened to a gull squawk as it descended to grab a fish, and then fly back up, out of sight.

She replayed the last few days, the conversations she'd had with Hillary, the gut feeling she had that she'd passed off as nerves, nothing more.

"But why Tim?" She could ask now. Of all the men on the Cape, why would her beautiful cousin have given him a second look?

"I wish I had a better answer," Hillary said. "But I'm in my thirties. I'm single. I don't particularly love my job but it's still demanding. I don't even have time for a dog and I really want one." She was crying now, and she laughed through her tears. "My job is a good one, but it doesn't inspire me. I haven't dated anyone in, like, two years. And my best friend moved away."

Caroline frowned deeply, even though she knew Hillary wasn't trying to blame her.

"I started wondering if this was all there would ever be for me. Maybe I should have done what you did. Moved. Started over."

"It's not all it's cracked up to be," Caroline said, feeling bad if she'd implied otherwise as a way to prove to the world, to Tim, and maybe even to herself, that she was okay.

But she was okay. More than okay. Being back in Harmony Cove. That was the missing link, and it had been here all along.

Hillary stopped crying long enough to look confused. "But you always said leaving town was the best decision you ever made."

"The best decision I ever made was coming back here," Caroline said, knowing in her heart that it was true. "I guess I was trying to convince myself that I wasn't lonely. Or homesick. Because I definitely convinced myself that I could never come home. My pride got in the way. My hurt feelings. My fear, I suppose. It held me back from what I loved most. From whom I loved most."

"Don't be so hard on yourself," Hillary said, linking her arm. "I've held myself back, too. Working that job for ten years with no advancement or end in sight. Not taking a risk, or listening to what would make me happy. Instead, committing to the first guy who'd paid me a little attention in a while, even though I knew that it was wrong. For so many reasons."

"That's why you stopped calling," Caroline said with a nod of understanding.

"I knew if I told you I was hanging out with him, I couldn't justify it. When he proposed... Well, I was shocked. I thought we were just having a bit of fun, and it was nice, you know, having someone other than my sisters or cousins or mother to go out to dinner with every once in a while. Most of our friends from school have all settled down by now."

Caroline nodded. "I understand."

"When he asked me to marry him, my entire life seemed to pass before my eyes, and all I could think of was that this might be the only proposal I would ever get. Or that it could be years before another one came along. That this was my chance to have the wedding of my dreams, the husband, the kids. The dog." Hillary pulled a tissue from her pocket and blew her nose. "But then I didn't even care about the wedding. And I started having a hard time picturing that future with Tim in it."

"You can still have all those things," Caroline told her. "And more."

"Oh, I am going to get a dog," Hillary announced firmly, then grinned. "Like, tomorrow."

"Will you let me take it for walks when you do get one?" Caroline asked hopefully.

Hillary stared at her in confusion. "Don't you have to get back to Philly?"

Caroline shook her head. "I have everything I need right here in Harmony Cove, and I happen to know that you do, too."

"Because I'm getting a dog?" Hillary asked skeptically.

"Because you took a risk," Caroline said. "It didn't work out. But that doesn't mean that you have to stop reaching for the life you always wanted."

"What are you getting at?" Hillary asked slowly.

Caroline thought of the idea that had been in the back of her mind all week, of the future she envisioned for her cousin and best friend, even if it hadn't been the one she was planning.

"Sheila at the flower shop is going out of business. And I think you would be the perfect person to take over."

"Me?" Hillary looked stunned, but a slow smile curved her mouth just as quickly. "I do like flowers."

"And you are extremely creative," Caroline said.

"And I don't love my job," Hillary said.

"And I do need a florist I can trust if I'm going to be planning events here in Harmony Cove," Caroline said as her smile grew. "And a family discount wouldn't hurt, either."

"Wait." Hillary halted to stare at her. Her big eyes shone with hope for the first time since Caroline had returned to town, and she knew then and there that her cousin was going to be all right.

They both were.

"Am I really doing this?" Hillary asked a little breathlessly.

"Am I?" Caroline laughed. "But isn't that what makes life exciting? Instead of letting these setbacks knock us down, we can pick ourselves back up. Start fresh. The Reynolds brothers don't get to dictate how we spend the rest of our lives."

Hillary gave her a funny look. "Not even Lucas? I was kind of thinking that you two had something going on. I mean, everyone did. Your kiss did make the Harmony Happenings column this morning."

"What?" Caroline now understood what her sisters were getting at, but instead of being amused, she felt overwhelmed with sadness.

She'd thought that she did have a connection with Lucas. Maybe a lasting one. But she'd been wrong.

Only unlike when she'd been wrong before, this time, she wasn't going to let it take her off course. This time, she was going to take back her life, the one she'd always wanted, and give herself her own happy ending.

If anyone deserved it, it was her and Hillary.

Unlike the last time Tim decided to bail on his bride, he didn't jump on the first ferry. Instead, he invited Lucas out for drinks at a bar two towns over, which was probably for the best given that both of them were persona non grata in Harmony Cove and probably would be for a while.

If not forever.

"I think I'll go back to Boston soon," Tim told him. "One of us should probably head up the corporate office."

If they still had a business come Monday, Lucas thought grimly.

"If I didn't know better, I'd say that you were more beat up about this than I am," Tim remarked, and Lucas slanted him a glare.

"The fact that you don't feel bad about calling off your wedding is hardly something to boast about," he replied, peeling the label off his bottle.

"Hillary is fine with it," Tim said. "If anything, I'd say she's relieved. She didn't really want to marry me any more than I wanted to marry her. We just got caught up in things."

Lucas took a slow sip of his drink. Maybe it was true, and part of him believed that it was. Still, he wished Tim wouldn't take it quite so lightly.

"Honestly, I think having Caroline in town made Hillary realize what she really wanted from life, and it wasn't me." Tim shrugged, but there was a sadness in his eyes. "They have a great family. Their lives are full."

The implication was that the Reynoldses' lives were not, even when up until recently, Lucas would have argued that his was.

"I always thought that you were happy having your freedom," he commented.

"I value it, but that doesn't mean I don't get lonely sometimes," Tim said with a half smile. "I just need to remind myself not to let my need for companionship lead to promises that I can't fulfill."

"No more proposals, then?" Lucas was skeptical but hopeful.

"Don't worry," Tim said with a laugh. "The next time I make a mess of my life, you don't need to pick up after me. But...thank you for doing so. Then. Now."

"Always," Lucas said gruffly, then took another swig of his beer.

"Some people are the marrying kind," Tim mused. "And some aren't."

Lucas nodded. They both knew which category their family fell into.

"I told you yesterday that I was over Caroline, and I am, but that doesn't mean I don't want the best for her," Tim suddenly said. "Or you."

Lucas felt his mouth go dry, but Tim wasn't finished speaking yet.

"Watching her this past week, it was clear that she had

fallen for someone else. And that my brother had fallen in love for the first time in his life," he finished with a big grin. "And, knowing you, the *only* time."

First and only. That sounded about right. He'd been there, done that, and made a huge mistake. He'd hurt someone he cared about. Just like Tim had done. Like his parents did, over and over. The Reynolds curse. There was no breaking the pattern.

"Caroline is an amazing woman," Tim said. "One of us should be so lucky as to have her. But only one of us deserves her."

"Oh, I don't think Caroline will want anything to do with me after today," Lucas replied with a shake of the head, but there was a pull in his chest, a longing that he'd never felt before, for something that he desperately wanted, even though he'd always thought he never would.

For something he now wasn't so sure he could live without.

"Why? Because of what I did?" Tim shrugged it off. "You're not me, Lucas. You're the complete opposite of me."

"Oh, I know." Lucas managed to laugh. "I don't have enough digits to count our differences."

"Not like that," Tim said. "You...you are the marrying kind, Lucas."

He pulled a sharp breath, then lifted his beer.

Maybe he was. Or maybe he just wished he could be.

Fifteen

Caroline's father was standing at the kitchen counter when she came downstairs the next morning. She halted, unsure what his presence meant, but just as quickly she hurried over and wrapped her arms around his waist, holding him tight. She rested her head on his shoulder, just like she'd done when she was younger, breathing in the sweet smell of coffee and mint toothpaste.

"Did you..." Caroline couldn't deny the hope in her voice, and she hoped that she wasn't jinxing anything by asking. Her mother had insinuated as much yesterday, but she needed to hear the confirmation from her father, too.

"Move back in?" He winked and then poured a cup of coffee and handed it to her before making one for himself.

"Oh, Dad." Caroline felt her eyes fill with tears of relief and happiness because she could tell by the way his entire face lit up that she was looking at a man still very much in love.

"What is it, honey?" her father asked, his brows pinching when he saw the tears in her eyes.

She shook her head, not wanting to ruin this moment for him, what should be a joyous occasion—and what was.

Her parents were back together. Love had prevailed, and maybe it would even last.

She hoped it would last. But there was no guarantee. And that was still a painful thing to accept.

"It's nothing," she said a little breathlessly. "I'm just happy for you, is all. You and Mom. Annie and Sean. It's almost enough to make me think that sometimes love does last."

"Sometimes?" Her father raised an eyebrow. "Do you mean that you don't believe in love anymore, Caroline?"

Caroline could only shrug, but she knew that her father saw right through her. She couldn't hide anymore. Not in Philadelphia. Not here in this house. Not from the people who she loved.

"I'm not sure that love exists for me," she admitted, sparking a sharp intake of breath from her father, whose expression folded before he took her back into his arms.

"How can you say that?" he asked, letting her go but leaving his hands on her shoulders. "You have me. Your mother. Your sisters. Always. Not to mention a handful of cousins and some loveable but eccentric aunts."

The twinkle returned to his blue eyes, pulling a wan smile from her.

"I mean romantic love," she said. "I never had to doubt your love."

"And you never will." He sighed and then lifted his

coffee from the counter, taking a long, pensive sip. "Your mother never did, either, for what it's worth. I never stopped loving her, even when we were having problems. But that's how I knew how much I loved her, I suppose. Because I never stopped fighting for her, even when we were living apart. My heart was always here, in this home, in the life we made together."

Caroline nodded, knowing that it was true. That she'd been right not to doubt their commitment to each other. To hold out hope that if any two people could stand the test of time, they could.

"Love isn't easy," her father said simply. "People let you down, but they also surprise you in the most wonderful ways. But if you're not willing to open your heart, then you'll close yourself off from all the possibilities that life can bring you."

"I guess I'm tired of being disappointed," Caroline said with a heavy sigh. She looked into the contents of her mug. Even a fresh cup of coffee couldn't lift her spirits today.

"What Tim did was awful," her father said firmly. "To you, and to Hillary. But don't you see, honey? What you had with him was...something...but I'm not sure that looking back, you would call it love."

"I thought I was in love at the time," Caroline said slowly. "Now, though, I'm not so sure. Tim was fun, and in many ways, he was the opposite of me, and I liked that because it was exciting. And familiar, given how long we were together."

"But?" Her father knew her so well. "What made you

realize that your feelings weren't what you thought? Because of what happened?"

Caroline thought about it and then shook her head. She knew the answer, she just wasn't ready to admit it yet. To him. To herself.

"I guess it took feeling right about someone else to understand just how wrong things were between me and Tim."

What she had with Tim was exciting and youthful, a relationship built on a shared past.

But a shared future was something he couldn't give her in the end. And one that she now couldn't imagine working out, either.

"Lucas Reynolds is a fine young man," her father said, snapping her attention back to him. Unable to completely hide his smile, he said, "I may not run the newspaper anymore, but that doesn't mean I'm able to resist my sister's column, and she had quite a bit to say you and that young man in yesterday's edition."

Caroline groaned, but her father wasn't finished.

"She had quite a bit to say today, too. About a certain hotel that may no longer be built."

Caroline frowned. "What? But why?"

"According to Marcy and her sources, the Reynolds men haven't lived up to their reputation. They pitched a family resort, and that's what the investors were counting on."

Caroline thought back to her many conversations with Lucas, how excited he'd been about the hotel, and why. It wasn't just about the money to him, or even the business, it was about starting a new life and undoing past wrongs, right here in the town that he loved.

"I knew that he had some important people coming to the wedding," she started, thinking now of how she'd accused him of having his own interest in making sure this wedding was successful. "Would they really pull their money if Tim didn't go through with the wedding?"

Her father shrugged. "To hear Marcy tell it, it's very possible. She's already come up with some potential other uses for the land, each one more outlandish than the next! I don't think anyone needs a zoo in Harmony Cove."

Caroline would usually laugh at this, but today she couldn't.

Lucas had given Tim his blessing, knowing what it would cost him. And even though she knew she should be furious, she found that she couldn't be.

Because Lucas's heart had been in the right place.

It always had been.

"You know the reason why some love doesn't last, Caroline?" her father asked gently. When she shook her head, he said, "Because someone stopped fighting for it."

She gave her father a kiss on the cheek. "I've missed these pep talks, Dad."

"And I've missed you," he said with a shine in his eyes when she pulled back.

"And I've missed you both," Caroline's mother said as she rounded the corner. She gave each of them a heartfelt smile, letting it linger on her husband for a moment.

"I think that's my cue to get dressed," Caroline said. "I...

think I'll take a walk." She needed to be near the water, to feel the salty breeze fill her lungs and clear her head.

And maybe unclutter her heart.

"There's something we wanted to ask you before you left," her mother said.

"Oh, Mom," Caroline said, giving both of her parents a big grin. "I'm not going anywhere. I'm staying right here, where I belong."

"That makes two of us," her dad said, reaching out to take his wife's hand.

"You mean you're not going back to Philly?" Her mother's eyes misted.

"Only to pack," Caroline said.

"But not today?" her mother asked hopefully.

Caroline shrugged. "It doesn't have to be today... Why?"

"We were going to ask you to push your flight off until tomorrow." Sharon looked up at her husband, who gave her a nod. "We've already talked to Sandra and Hillary first thing this morning, but now we need to talk to you. We know it's short notice, but we also know how hard you've worked this past week, and, well, it was going to be a beautiful wedding..."

Caroline sighed. "It was." She'd made sure of that herself.

With a little help, she couldn't help but think...

"And it would be a shame to see it go to waste," her father said.

Caroline narrowed her eyes at her parents. "What is this? What are you getting at?"

"It's a beautiful day for a wedding." Her mother

beamed, waving her arm toward the window, where seagulls swooped against the cloudless blue sky. "That is if you wouldn't mind helping to put it all back together again?"

"But..." Caroline thought of all the calls she had made yesterday afternoon, the work that had gone into undoing the very plans she had made. The flowers. The cake. The rental tables and chairs.

"We'll have everything here, at the house," Sharon explained. "Our family home, where Mitch and I started our lives, and where we will finish them."

"Mom." Caroline brushed at a tear as it slid down her cheek. "Oh, Mom, I wish I could help. But the flowers and the cake—"

"Are all stored at the café and the bakery," her mother finished. "Your father got the idea last night, and made a few calls of his own."

Mitch winked. "And you all worried about what I would do in my retirement."

Caroline laughed. "Does Annie know? And the others?"

Her mother nodded. "We called them all first thing. Everyone knows. And they're all ready to help. But we couldn't do this without you, Caroline. Will you stay?"

Caroline opened her arms wide and folded both of her parents into them. "I'll stay. And I'll help. And I'll make this the best wedding ever."

And this time, she didn't have any worries about whether or not it would actually happen. Because this time, she knew, that the two people who would be exchanging the vows were not just in love, and not just committed, but meant to be.

And that maybe there was someone out there meant for her, too.

Lucas ended the call with Chef Isaac, knowing that he should feel satisfied with the arrangement they'd made in the end and secure in the fact that their relationship was intact, even if the man may not be opening a signature restaurant at the hotel after all, because there very likely wouldn't be a hotel at all.

He had planned to wait until Monday to deal with Wallace, but after a fitful night of sleep, Lucas had woken early, gone into the office, and then hurried back into town around midmorning, hoping that Wallace was enjoying the Bayview Inn's breakfast buffet before facing the traffic back into Boston.

He found his top investor and his wife sitting outside the bakery, at a small table, sipping coffee and sharing a plate of pastries. His pulse quickened even as he slowed his pace, not wanting to disturb this peaceful moment, but knowing that sometimes the truth had to be faced, no matter how difficult it was.

"Wallace," he said, drawing the attention of the older man.

He braced himself for a deep scowl, or a brief scolding, but instead, Wallace's wide face broke out into a grin. "Lucas! We were just enjoying the most delicious breakfast after taking a long stroll along the bay. I was just telling my wife that I could get used to this lifestyle. I see why people enjoy coming to Harmony Cove."

Lucas stared at the man and his wife, who were smiling pleasantly, trying to make sense of this unexpected good mood.

Had they not shown up to the wedding after all? Had they not been aware that it had been called off? That Tim Reynolds had proven himself not to be the marrying kind. That his reputation was intact, and not in line with the image the hotel was selling.

"You just missed your brother," Wallace said, and now Lucas froze.

After a brief pause, he managed to say, "You saw Tim?"

"He's a charming fellow," Wallace said with a chuckle. "And he certainly looks up to you."

Lucas's eyebrows shot up. He opened his mouth but found he couldn't speak because he didn't know what to say. Not when he didn't know what Tim had said. Not when he'd never stopped to think of what his brother might think of him—only what he thought of his kid brother.

Shame washed over him for a moment as Wallace continued to grin.

"Seems that the boy might have a lot to learn about love," the man went on, sliding a glance at his wife, "but he certainly understands the meaning of family. Told me that there was no one better to run this project than you, and he listed all the reasons why. He said that a lot of people had let him down in his life, and he'd done the same. But that he always knew that you'd never disappoint him. Or anyone else for that matter."

Lucas's throat felt tight. If only that were true. Because he had let someone down.

Even though it was the last thing he'd wanted to do.

Wallace leaned back in his chair. "You remind me a lot of myself, Lucas."

Lucas nodded. "I'm a man of my word, sir. And that hotel—"

But Wallace held up a hand. "I'm not talking about the hotel, Lucas. I'm talking about you. You and me, we're family men, Lucas."

Lucas's throat felt tight. He could only nod in response. It was perhaps the best compliment anyone had ever paid him even if he'd never seen himself that way.

Only wanted to. And wished to.

"You have a real vision for that hotel and I know you'll make it a success," Wallace said confidently. "Because it's not all about business to you. It never was."

Lucas let those words sink in as he left Wallace and his wife to enjoy their breakfast and then stopped by the harbor to look out at the boats and farther up the coastline, where he could just make out the property where his big hotel would be built.

Wallace was right. It wasn't just about the hotel. It was about what it represented. A dream that was always out of reach.

One that was worth fighting for.

∽

The guest list for the vow renewal started with family but grew as word of mouth spread, thanks in large part to Marcy, who had taken the liberty of running an announcement in her gossip column in the morning's edition, and even Annie hadn't tried to stop her.

"We knew you wouldn't go back to Philly," Annie said triumphantly as they finished decorating the backyard. Kathy had brought over the cake, which was waiting inside, and the food for the reception should be arriving at any moment.

"I couldn't abandon all this," Caroline said, feeling a sense of pride in what they'd accomplished. "Or all of you."

Or herself. And what she wanted most.

She glanced backward at the house, wishing that she'd thought to make a checklist, and going through a mental one instead. Her mother had promised that the food was under control, but Caroline didn't like the thought of her working through her own vow renewal.

"Mom said the food was on the way," she said, even though she hadn't seen any sign of Delia from the café. "Let me go check."

She hurried across the lawn and up the back porch steps, but her hand dropped from the screen door when she saw a familiar car pull to a stop in the driveway. It wasn't the café van she'd been waiting for—or any vehicle that she'd expected.

It was an expensive black SUV, much like the one that had parked beside hers at the restaurant in Chatham.

Before she had time to contemplate this, the front door opened and Lucas stepped out. He looked around for a minute at the activity taking place in the backyard, and then, noticing her, held up a hand.

With a hammering heart, Caroline glanced at the door to the house, knowing that she could run inside, safe in the comfort of her own home, where he couldn't get to her, talk to her, stop her.

But she'd been hiding for too long.

Another vehicle crunched along the gravel, pulling Caroline's attention along with Lucas's.

"I came bearing a gift!" Lucas called out, motioning to the white van behind him where Chef Isaac and his crew were already unpacking trays of food. After a brief exchange with Lucas, the team wearing catering uniforms carried everything to the porch, looking at Caroline expectantly.

She stared at them for a moment and then at Lucas, who remained a safe distance from the house, watching her. With a nod, she opened the screen door so they could pass inside, still confused even as Lucas slowly made his way up the steps.

He was dressed casually, for him, at least, in khaki pants and a linen button-down. And even though he seemed to have had something to do with Chef Isaac's arrival, it wasn't the caterers that he was focused on.

It was her.

"Your mother shouldn't have to cater her own wedding," Lucas explained. "And I already talked to Molly this morning."

Molly. Caroline didn't think she had it in her to be so sly. She would have to have a word with her youngest sister.

But not now. Because right now, she needed to have a word with the man standing before her.

She glanced around the crowded yard, moving around the side of the house, where they could talk discreetly—unless Marcy decided to crack the kitchen window.

"How did you know about the change of plans?" she asked, searching his face for some understanding of why he was here, especially after the way they'd left things yesterday.

Lucas gave her a crooked smile. "I think your aunt Marcy made sure everyone knew."

Despite herself, Caroline laughed, then stopped. She was supposed to be mad at this man. And she was mad. Very mad. And hurt. And confused.

And...maybe...in love.

"Thank you," she said, meaning it. "For the chef. I...take it you two are still on good terms?"

His nod was curt, but there was a fleeting smile that passed over his face. "He's agreed to be the chef at the hotel."

Her eyebrows shot up. "So it's still happening? Your investor didn't pull out after all?" When he looked confused, she added, "Marcy also mentioned you in today's article."

But Lucas didn't seem bothered. Instead, he grinned broadly, but only for a moment. "Believe it or not, we didn't end up losing any investors. I just...hope that I didn't lose whatever was happening between us, Caroline."

She pulled in a breath against the pounding of her heart. It would be so easy to end things now, to walk back to the safety of her childhood home and the loving arms of her family, to shield herself from potential disappointment or worse.

But she knew what that future would look like. It might be safe, but it would be lonely.

"Well, I'm sure you have a lot to do to get ready for the event," Lucas said, turning to go.

"Wait," Caroline blurted. He turned to her, surprised. "You should stay. You brought all this food. And we know how delicious it will be. And...it's going to be a great wedding. Or vow renewal. Or...party."

"Or...commitment ceremony," Lucas said, giving her a slow grin. "You know, when I read about your parents finding their way back to each other, I had this feeling that today was going to be a really good day."

She stared at him, unsure of where he was going with this. "Oh?"

"I didn't have parents like yours growing up," Lucas said. "And I only knew your parents through Tim. But wow... what a dream, you know? That's what I always thought it was, just a dream. But lately, now...well, I'm starting to believe it's more than that. That maybe it's possible."

Caroline swallowed hard, not daring to speak, because she knew that if she did, she'd have to say that she agreed with him. That she agreed with him about a lot of things.

"I thought, after yesterday, that you really didn't believe in love. For yourself. Or your brother," she finally said.

He stared at her, then nodded, just once. "I stood by my brother yesterday out of more than loyalty. I did it because I love the guy, and I knew that he didn't love your cousin the way he should, just like he didn't love you the way he should have." His eyes darkened. "I'm sorry if I let you down, Caroline. It was the last thing I wanted to do."

"You almost let yourself down," she said. "You almost lost your hotel. Your future. Everything you'd planned."

"What I planned was a life not much unlike my father's, even though I didn't see it. Sure, my business ideas took a different form, but I was still making work my entire life. And I don't want to do that anymore." He took a step closer to her, and this time, she didn't step back. "I never really dared to ask myself what I wanted. I just told myself what I could and couldn't have and lived within those rules. It felt safer that way. More secure. And more...steady, I suppose."

She nodded. She understood. Not for the same reasons, perhaps, but still, she knew what it felt like to believe that love was only for other people.

And she knew what it felt like to let love in.

"I thought I didn't want love. But I do want it, Caroline," he said. "I just never believed in it before, not until you."

Tears brimmed in her eyes, and she didn't trust herself to speak. But actions, she knew from experience, often meant so much more than words.

She reached out, slipping her hand into his, and squeezing it tight until he did the same.

"They're coming!" Annie said, poking her head over the hydrangea bushes. "Hurry up and get to your place!"

Caroline looked back at Lucas. "You'll stay?"

"I'm not dressed..." he started to say but she just laughed.

"You're perfect just as you are. Besides, it's all family here."

And it was.

Smoothing the sundress that Molly had lent her, the one that coordinated with the casual but pretty dresses her other sisters wore, Caroline joined the three other Baker girls at the makeshift altar, under the garden trellis that was cascading with pink roses.

Val's client had shown up with her violin, and she began to play as the porch door opened and Sharon and Mitch Baker stepped outside, hand in hand, no longer a young couple full of hope and dreams but an older version of their former selves, full of memories, and maybe even more in love than ever.

Caroline glanced at Annie, knowing that if she dared to look at Molly, she'd tear up, but she saw that Annie wasn't watching her parents at this moment. She was looking at Sean.

And for the first time, Caroline was no longer worried for her sister. She was happy. Happy because her sister had dared to take a second chance on love, just like their parents.

Just like herself.

They'd opened their hearts. They'd dared to believe.

Caroline's gaze drifted to Lucas, seated in the back row, three behind Marcy, who was sobbing into a pink tissue, and beside Kathy, who gave Caroline a not-so-discreet thumbs-up sign and then wandered over to Hillary, who watched wistfully as the Bakers made their way down the aisle, not for what might have been, but rather, for what still could be.

It wasn't the wedding that any of them expected and certainly not the one that Caroline had planned. But then, sometimes the path to happily-ever-after had some unexpected bumps and turns and wonderful surprises along the way.

Keep Reading

A Hometown Holiday
Harmony Cove Book Three

It's been years since the entire Baker family has gathered for Christmas, and youngest sister Molly has been counting the days until their beloved traditions begin—but she hadn't been counting on an early Christmas surprise.

When her mother announces her sudden retirement (and an impromptu second honeymoon) and leaves Molly to run their popular café during the holiday rush, there is more than a little reason for panic. Molly is determined to uphold her family legacy but when the town's newest Grinch criticizes her efforts, she begins to worry that this Christmas won't just be disappointing, it will also be a disaster.

Eric Hansen may have lost his late mother's restaurant, but he hopes to honor her by returning to Harmony Cove—and making peace with her best friend's daughter. He came to town to escape all thoughts of Christmases past, but Molly might just have him believing in a brighter future.

As twinkle lights glow and old memories resurface, Molly and Eric find themselves drawn together by family ties...and a little Christmas magic. And in a town full of second chances, they discover that while time-honored traditions can be treasured, sometimes the new ones we create are the best gift of all.

Read Now!

About the Author

Olivia Miles is a two-time *USA Today* bestselling author of heartwarming women's fiction and small town romance. After growing up in New England, she now lives on the shore of Lake Michigan with her family and an adorable pair of dogs.

Visit www.OliviaMilesBooks.com for more.

www.ingramcontent.com/pod-product-compliance
Lightning Source LLC
LaVergne TN
LVHW030318070526
838199LV00069B/6502